TRACING the BONES

TRACING the BONES

a novel

Elise A. Miller

author of Star Craving Mad

SparkPress, a BookSparks imprint
A Division of SparkPoint Studio, LLC

Published by SparkPress, a BookSparks imprint,
A division of SparkPoint Studio, LLC
Tempe, Arizona, USA, 85281
www.gosparkpress.com

Published 2016
Printed in the United States of America

ISBN: 978-1-940716-48-0 (pbk)
ISBN: 978-1-940716-49-7 (e-bk)
Library of Congress Control Number: 2015959047

Cover design © Julie Metz, Ltd./metzdesign.com
Author photo © Christine Dorian
Formatting by Katherine Lloyd, The DESK

To Ry and Frankie, and Bryan
for always

Darkness within darkness.
The gateway to all understanding.

—*The Tao Te Ching*

Dance with me, across the sea
We can feel the motion of a thousand dreams...

—*The Thompson Twins*

Chapter 1

*L*ess than a minute after I've torn myself from the sacred womb of unconsciousness, Neil has taken over the bed, his pale form splayed like a puff-pastry Jesus on a sweat-soaked cotton cross. He snores softly, an escaped goose feather woven into his silvery stubble. In the bathroom I grab a pen from between the pages of his crossword puzzle book, pull an *Us Weekly* subscription card from the trash and scribble, *Dissatisfied housewife dying slow death in suburbia. Swallows contaminated Xanax. Turns into giant stinkbug.*

Downstairs the Christmas tree greets me, still lit from the night before, threatening to ignite. In the dining room Neil's cuckoo clock, salvaged from his boyhood, marks each moment with its faux wood maple leaf pendulum. When he first hung it I thought it looked hip. Now I just want it to shut the fuck up. My mother put it nicely. She waltzed in one evening, took one look at it and said, "Oh, so now you have a goyishe tchotchke to announce the passage of time. Aren't the children enough for you?" I'd never thought about it like that before, but from then on, every time I looked at Sam, my oldest, I'd see in his tender years the amount of time that had passed since my life included a luxurious autonomy and freedom, a life devoted to finding myself, uncovering meaning and purpose, experimenting with creative career paths—actress, interior designer, slam poet—versus my life now, which is devoted to finding the time to make a phone call, take a shower, stare out a window and sit on the toilet without someone barging in to show me his latest ninja move.

The sinkful of crusty dishes spawns a kernel of anxiety in my gut that radiates until it throbs against my skull and the base of my spine—my soul groping for an escape hatch. On a napkin I scrawl, *In a post-apocalyptic America, mid-life disillusionment cross-pollinates with stale gluten-free bread crumbs, mutating into parasitic virus, infecting millions of serotonin-depleted moms, creating race of killer housewife zombies.*

Writing like this, on scraps of garbage, has become my pet venture since remembering how much I used to love writing, and realizing with disturbing clarity that I hate cleaning, knitting, homeroom parenting, gardening and scrapbooking. I grew up in the city, was never a cheerleader, sorority girl, or joiner. I scowled more than I smiled. If you were a casting agent you'd see that I was a Wednesday Addams, or Winona Ryder circa *Beetlejuice,* thrust into middle age.

Pondering my marketable type I notice something new outside the window staked in front of the neighbor's house—a For Sale sign. Its owner died over the summer from lung cancer. I'd see her every now and then toting an oxygen tank in her driveway. There's a rusty old swing set in her yard. No one ever touched it, so one day we asked if we could have it for the kids. The old lady clutched her throat and shot her chin in the air. She said, I keep it for my *grandchildren.* But her grandchildren never came. No one did. The swing set just sat there. It's sitting there still, home to a family of house wrens.

I grab the coffee, measure five scoops into the machine. I need all the help I can get since the days are endless. The year, however, passes in a blur. I've Googled the expression but don't know its origins. One of those universal truths—*the days are long but the years are short.* So as the days, weeks and months congeal into taffy ribbons, calendar pages flutter in my hand's weary wake, and by the time my index finger depresses the start button on the coffee maker, it is January. Sprinkled around the house are scraps of paper scribbled with half-sentences, character sketches and aborted story ideas. The For Sale sign next door is still there. I've watched as various young couples and families have come to consider the bland four-bedroom with the weathered aluminum siding.

Chloe is still lying in bed when I open her door in February. A handful of valentines from her kindergarten classmates litter the top of her Ikea cubbies. The snow outside has wizened like an old crone, glinting under the white sky. I pluck a pair of Sleeping Beauty underpants, a floral print dress I bought on clearance at Target, and a pair of striped leggings from the neighborhood consignment shop.

"Good morning," I say, easing into the bottom bunk.

My daughter does not stir.

I soak up her warmth, shove my nose between her lips and huff her morning breath like glue. Her hair explodes into a nest of tangles. "The elves were here again last night," I whisper in her ear, peeling back the covers. I silently appraise my daughter's body in her fairy nightgown—her long legs, innate elegance, perfectly round little bottom, grubby little feet and hands. I pray that when she is a teenager I will not be cruel to her for being more beautiful than I ever was. I hope instead that I will continue nearly worshipping her, without giving in to her every whim.

I reach for the hem of her nightgown.

"Mommy get off me!" She whines.

"Come on sweetie. Let's get it over with."

She cracks an eye, spies today's outfit nestled in my lap. "I don't want that dress," she says.

"Then pick out one you want," I say already gritting my teeth.

She yanks the covers over her head. I sigh at the ceiling and then survey the room. Her bookshelves ooze chewed board books that need to be culled, donated, recycled. The walls are graffitied with fluorescent pink highlighter. Stick-on earrings dot the floor— shiny bumps on the old pine planks, long forgotten. Is it a cruel joke that they refuse to stay on her ears, resulting in earsplitting heartbreak, yet I'll have to use an X-acto to pry them off the floor? I cup her heel through the stained quilt and whisper *nam myoho renge kyo*—'I devote my life to the law of the Lotus Sutra.' I don't really, but the chant calms me. For a moment anyway.

Sam emerges from his room across the hall in March, a few days after his seventh birthday, his nostrils already flaring. Outside the snow has given way to mud and yellow grass. Tender shoots get a thrashing from the wind that whips circles around our stone farmhouse. Crocuses push their purple heads through the hard-packed soil, fearless leaders in springtime's parade.

"I don't want to go!" he wails and falls to the floor, still in his Star Wars pajamas. Sam's teachers call him gifted—a perfection-ist with a sensitive soul. I call him exhausting. Maybe his teachers could come over one day and witness his sensitivity—when it's time to wake up, get his homework done, sit down to dinner, take a bath... They can drag him through his day, his sticky fingers gripping their ankles while I take a nap. I know I'm supposed to appreciate the miracle of my children and believe me these chil-dren were wanted and planned for. And there are times when I well up with a love so vast and fathomless that I could eat them. Usually those times are when they're asleep, or when someone else is watching them. My sweet baby boy, it seems, has grown into a prickly porcupine.

Sam arches his back, balls his hands into fists and shrieks at the ceiling, emitting a sound that could annoy the dead. I stare at the wall above his writhing body where a cluster of framed baby photos mocks me, like the one where his infant socks are so big they look like drawstring pouches. Then I grab a ribbon of receipt from Bed, Bath & Beyond from the sideboard and scribble across it—*Devil's spawn possesses mother. Takes her to the underworld where he builds a boat and uses her femurs for oars.*

Chloe pipes up from her room. "Mommy, he's hurting my ears!" she cries.

"Get dressed right now," I hiss.

Sam's keening shreds the morning. When he finally settles down to a bowl of Cheerios, blotch-faced and snot-glossed, I chase Chloe around the house with a brush. I give up on the fifth lap when she runs face-first into the guest room door. I hold her on my lap, soothing her while she wails so loudly I might go deaf in one ear. Fat silvery tears roll down her chapped cheeks and I kiss away every one.

By the time I open the front door, the bruise on Chloe's nose is turning green as April rain plummets outside. It muddies the stone pathway that leads to the driveway, pounding the tulips until they bow their fleshy heads and kiss the ground. We head out, suited up in plasticky rain gear. Beside the tree the For Sale sign boasts a jumbo SOLD sticker. I vaguely wonder who our new neighbors will be as I prod the kids into the minivan.

As the doors slide shut, the rain evaporates. Chloe's bruise has faded. Her nose is almost as pink as the magnolia petals littering the sidewalks, heralding the arrival of May. The Scotch broom that abuts the side of our house accessorizes with tiny yellow flowers that shiver in the breeze.

I back out of the driveway, past the rusted container sitting in front of the house next door, overflowing with construction debris—great gray ribbons of aluminum siding, antique two-by-fours, frayed knob-and-tube wiring, the rusty old swing set. Tepid coffee spills down my chin. This jars my memory. I forgot to make sure the kids brushed their teeth. Chloe's hair is still a knotty mess. *Shit.*

In front of the school entrance Sam almost forgets his back-pack. When he retrieves it, he swings it into his sister's head hard enough to elicit tears. I glance at his feet just in time to see that his shoelaces are already untied. Chloe wails. *SHIT.*

"Have a good day, kids," I say. "And Sam—try not to breathe on anyone."

"What?" Sam says.

"Never mind."

He reaches into the car one more time to grab a Pokemon card from the floor.

"Leave it!" I snap and he drops it, mercifully. Usually I don't snap until Friday, but I can make an exception, just this once. I watch the kids trudge away, their backpacks sliding from their narrow shoulders. The car behind me honks. "Fuck off," I mutter under my breath, and drive away, nice and slow.

Back at home it's June. The morning glows chartreuse, edged with steel. The humidity has arrived and with it, the mosquitoes. The shadow over our homes continues to spread, cast by the neigh-bor's house.

In her driveway my new neighbor confers with a guy—the con-tractor, I presume—who must be a foot taller than she is, wearing Timberland work boots and a chunky gold watch. He's holding a scroll of blueprints and gesturing wildly at the house, punctuating his speech with sharky grins that indicate how much fun renovating must be for the wealthy. As she gestures back—I can almost hear her say, *Make it bigger!*—her shiny nails leave coral tracks in the air.

A shaggy-haired preschooler runs around them. A black Mer-cedes SUV—one of those boxy safari-looking ones—sits at the curb.

I exit the van, feeling a stab of pain in my spine as I offer an unreturned wave. My neighbor is one of Those Main Line Women, so wealthy she glows, so entitled she takes up two parking spaces at Whole Foods, where the lot is already cramped and hostile. She's so protected by her luxury goods that the filth and stink of the middle class cannot penetrate her designer fortress. I know I shouldn't judge, but she's standing next door to my house in a gauzy tunic and buttery soft-looking leather gladiator sandals, all skinny and laughing, with a hundred-and-thirty-thousand-dollar pile of steel parked at the curb. It's difficult to overlook such things.

The coffee is still at the same level in the pot so I know Neil hasn't woken up, nor does he have to, since his work day doesn't start until four. He works second shift, which ends at midnight. It was the only job he could get when we moved and it throws everything off—meals, weekends, his personality, sex. I pour myself a mug and sip the cold bitter stuff, reminding myself once again to breathe forgiveness into my cells because it still stings that my husband of more than a decade ran away for a long weekend last year, just after we signed the mortgage papers—his mid-life crisis off to a blistering start—in part thanks to an old bandmate who promised him the success he always longed for, in exchange for his soul.

The story is, Neil was a musician once upon a time. He played guitar and harmonized with a ruddy-faced, broad-shouldered girl named Cyndi Pruce. I'd always thought she was gay. Maybe it was a subconscious wish. Neil and Cyndi nearly broke through the household name barrier when their most popular song, *Your Ass Don't Look Fat in Those Jeans*, sold to a reality show about a formerly skinny celeb working her way through the most popular diets while living with three of her ex-boyfriends, one of whom was going to train her for a figure model competition. It would be aired on TLC. The trouble was, the former starlet took up with a Vegas hotelier and dropped a ton of weight from the cocaine he introduced her to. The show aired twice and then got canceled. Now the actress hosts some other reality show about recovering addicts and Neil manages the word processing department of a mid-level law firm in Philadelphia.

We left Brooklyn to start over, to cash in on our Park Slope shoebox—we traded it for a four-bedroom stone farmhouse in suburban Philadelphia with a yard, driveway, detached garage and vivid Japanese maple out front. Great schools, great shopping, and my mom lives nearby. She's almost eighty, and had just endured a cascade of surgeries—cataract operation, hip replacement, hysterectomy. She lives alone; my brother's out in the sticks, my sister works fourteen-hour shifts and I'm a glutton for punishment.

Cyndi Pruce nearly saved Neil from the suburban drudgery his life was fast becoming like a helicopter swooping in on a hiker about to be engulfed in a landslide. She told him there was another chance for another song on another show. The song was called *Is it Cheatin'*, about a guy who's obsessed with another woman. The show was called, aptly enough, *Cheaters*. Neil approached me dancing for joy. We both danced for joy at the prospect of his success finally arriving after so many years he spent playing dive bars with sticky floors, and rehearsing most weekends. Then he threw up (from nerves), kissed the kids and got in the car.

The deal fell through before twenty-four hours had passed and he came crawling back—*after* he and Cyndi spent the weekend fucking in a motel room, scoring extra credit for demonstrating the song's theme. He literally crawled up the steps to our house to confess his sins. He looked at me as if I was supposed to praise him for coming clean. "I can't lie to you," he'd said, clinging to my leg.

"But you can fuck your bandmate in a shitty motel?" I'd said. "You should be commended." Then I left him with the kids and blew two hundred dollars on a massage and mani-pedi in the Wynnewood shopping center. I had the sweet Vietnamese girl with the face mask paint my nails black, in remembrance of my urban past when I was unchained, back when Neil was pretty, with floppy blond hair and a flat stomach.

I spent the rest of that evening trying on three-hundred dollar dresses at Anthropologie in Wayne. I pocketed a beautiful hundred and eighteen dollar necklace, as if that would teach Neil a lesson. I put it on in the parking lot, no one the wiser. It was called a "Solemn Oath Strand," and it was a tiny bird's wing that looked to be carved of bone, with a blue string tied in a bow around it. It spoke to me. It inspired me to forget about the oath Neil and I made to each other and instead make a promise to myself—to always be true. Neil never says a thing when I wear it. And he knew enough to not mention my nails either, financial worrywart that he is.

My husband wept for days. He wrote me twenty apology poems, like this one—

If I could take it all back
If I could make it all gone
I'd unbreak the window
I'd rewind the dawn.
I'd be true to you always
I'd stay by your side
But I can't, and I'm so very sorry baby!
It's like we both died.

I thought about poisoning him. I could have used the seven-hundred-fifty-thousand his insurance would have paid. But I fed him safe, nontoxic food, fearing jail. And I took him back, fearing single motherhood, because for one thing, I am devoted to not traveling in my mother's maritally meandering footsteps. For another, I see what my divorced sister Jeannie goes through with her son Griffin on a daily basis—from child support, to a dick of an ex, to legal fees, and of course shuttling the kid back and forth between houses. It sends needles of terror through my veins. And this is saying nothing of what it would do to the kids. I happened to be happy when my parents divorced because it meant that I didn't have to run screaming from my belt-wielding temperamental— emphasis on the *mental*—father anymore. But Neil is not like my dad. He's good to the kids, and aside from his spectacular gaffe in sound judgment, he's good to me. When he's well rested anyway.

Neil and I slept in separate rooms for the first six months. Now we sleep in the same bed, but in separate universes. We have had sex *once* since the incident. It wasn't even hot angry sex. It was dutiful sex. Mutual masturbation. I should get ASSHOLE tattooed across my forehead—backward—so I can read it when I look in the mirror, which is not often anymore.

A saw blazes to life next door, snapping me out of my noxious woolgathering. A nail gun erupts. A massive delivery truck rumbles to the curb. On the back of a receipt I scribble, *Part-time single mother gets shiny new neighbor. Homicidal bloodbath ensues.* I smile as I count the ways.

From the kitchen window I glance once more at my chic new neighbor, just in time to see the larger-than-life contractor smack her on the ass. She rubs her stinging rear with one delicate hand and joke punches the contractor with the other. Then she looks around, her mouth open, all white teeth and glossed lips. Nice Ray Bans, I think, as he dives in for a kiss.

Chapter 2

Jeannie winces as she bends to sit on her double-thick recycled purple mat. "I broke my vagina," she says, not bothering to lower her voice, which on most occasions booms.

"Which one was this?" I ask, glancing around the room to see that the regulars at Sweat & Reverence do not flinch at my sister's bellowing pronouncements—they have been inoculated. Today it's just regulars, which I count as a blessing. The last time someone shushed her was two years ago. Jeannie got up, walked her mat over to the woman, set up shop and began chanting Hare Krishna until everyone joined in, including the shusher, who never did return for another class. Jeannie called it karma. The rest of us called it chutzpah. One guy called it insanity, but you could tell he was dazzled. I've grown to love my sister's mouth after a long, wintry adolescence of resentment. I used to think she was doing herself a disservice, but age and motherhood showed me the light—there's nothing like a bucket of ice-cold honesty to pour over someone's head when your formerly firm ass is getting kicked by a couple of overprotected ingrates.

"The real estate agent," she says. "The one from Match."

"Oh," I nod, remembering. This is the one who makes his killing selling Main Line mansions. Jeannie has some sort of magnetic appeal when it comes to rich men. The trouble is, they're always jerks. Her ex is an OB-GYN downtown. Jeannie found the texts—dozens of them between him and his girlfriend—while he was showering one night. It was the only place he didn't take his cell. Jeannie thinks he was too stupid to delete them. I think he wanted to be caught. He left it up to her to file for divorce. Didn't want to be the one to bring it up. Can't imagine why.

My sister and I, despite stylistic differences and a five-year age gap, have always been close. Jeannie protected me from my dad. She took the blame for things I was accused of—marking up the walls with pencil, forgetting to turn the basement light off, spilling an entire tube of Love's Baby Soft Powder on the new shag carpet. Jeannie and I have different fathers. Whereas mine was the belt-whipping bastard doctor, her father before was the absent, stingy workaholic who ran a fleet of soft pretzel carts downtown. Both dads caused our mother a rash of hospitalizations—doctor-supervised time-outs that were our mother's way of neglecting her responsibilities. The loony bin was her respite. Her holiday. She particularly loved painting pottery and arranging dried flowers, and she didn't bother taking the masking tape name tag off her hair dryer after her fourth stay. She knew she'd return sooner or later. Jeannie took care of me when our mother was gone. She made me Cream of Wheat and helped me with my homework. She took me to Kip's Delicatessen for cheeseburgers and milkshakes. Gave me quarters for the jukebox and didn't groan when I chose "Le Freak" or "Dancing Queen," even though Jeannie, like her twin brother Larry, prefers Zeppelin over disco every day of the week. Jeannie was the mother I'd never had, and I have always loved her above and beyond the sisterly standard. Our brother Larry is a different matter. But more on him later.

"And the Odious Testicle!" Jeannie bellows. "He just texted me—called me a money grubbing *whore*! He should talk!" Her salt-and-pepper ringlets dance around as the tan on her face, chest and shoulders deepens to maroon. "Meanwhile he's nickel-and-diming me about child support all the way to the courthouse while his new *wife*, with her plastic *tits*, drives to the *spa* in a *Hummer*."

"So gross," I say, surveying the room, watching the other students set up mats, blankets and meditation cushions in two neat rows facing each other, balling up sweatshirts, gathering tissues and setting water bottles of every conceivable pattern and color within reaching distance.

Jeannie runs her fingers through her hair, shakes her wrists, bracelets jangling, as if the Odious Testicle were a spider she could flick away. Then she closes her eyes and starts chanting. "*Om gam ganapataye namaha...*"

"What a suckbag," I say, noticing the physical effects of my older sister's stress and sleep deprivation—the purplish shadows under her eyes, the deepening crease between her brows, the lips thinner than I remember, set in a perpetual frown.

Jeannie opens her eyes, hugs her knees and stares at the floor beyond the edge of her yoga mat. "I'd better have some yogurt later. Cool my Pitta."

"Well, at least he reminds you why you left," I say, wishing I could conjure a sweet, sexy wealthy man for her, which is archaic I know. Or a windfall. But the man would keep her warmer at night.

"Yeah," she says. "I am so much happier now, you know?"

"Oh God yes," I say, hoping my tone doesn't betray my true perspective on the matter. My sister is strong but she's lonely. And exhausted, and still hurting from the shitty marriage she's working so hard to overcome.

"How's your back?" She rolls her head side to side, massaging her neck.

"Today? Sciaticky. Yesterday, more of a crippling spasm. I'm so sick of it."

"Are you ever going to get it X-rayed?"

"Neil gave me this book that says it's most likely psychosomatic." Subtext: *quit your whining.*

Jeannie's forehead crinkles. "Eve. Listen to me. Even if your pain is psychosomatic you still need to rule out the structural stuff."

"Lorelei thinks it's my *kula*," I say, wondering what the difference is at this point. Physical pain. Mental pain. Mystical, spiritual, existential pain.

"I don't get you. You've had this pain for years. What is wrong with a fucking X-ray?"

"Okay," I tell her. "I'll do it if you stop nagging me."

"And maybe get a clay facial. It will harness your *Vata*."

"Will you pay for it?" I ask, batting my eyes.

My sister gives me the *fuck off* face.

Lorelei enters the studio, her hard, tattooed body encased in Lululemon, and floats across the floor. "Namaste, everyone. Good to see you on this wet morning," she says, setting up a meditation cushion beside the small dancing Shiva statue. "I don't know about you, but when it's raining I run through the falling drops, in order to get somewhere dry, somewhere I think I will be more pleasant, in the future."

The students, about twelve of us in all, murmur in agreement. Jeannie eats Lorelei's sermons with a spoon. Me, I come for the physical. Jeannie says I need to open to the possibilities. I say I need to figure out how to perform a handstand in the middle of the room.

"Now everyone, take a *dry*, comfortable seat. Spread your sitting bones wide. Elongate your spine and breathe into your lower ribs, stretching tall." Lorelei does this along with us, bundling her purple dreadlocks behind her back as she settles.

"Let your hands rest on your thighs... close your eyes... and enjoy your breath."

The front door opens. I hate it when people show up late. I was just beginning to relax. Lorelei excuses herself while the rest of us sit still with our eyes closed. Moments later our teacher returns with a fresh student who turns out to be my new neighbor. She looks a little too dazzling for my taste, in her clingy black sportsbra and short shorts. Lorelei directs her our way and she squeezes in between Jeannie and me.

"Sorry about that," she says to us, unrolling her mat. "I hate it when others are late."

"No problem," I say, angling to get a look at her cleavage as she squats before us, lining up the corners of her mat with the bamboo floor slats.

Jeannie shrugs. "Eh," she says and gives me a look that says, *what a tart.*

My sexy lithe neighbor shoots Jeannie a look that says, *the fuck I am, bitch*, which I find hilarious. Then she leaps and twirls in slow-motion landing in lotus position. She prayers her hands and bows to my sister. "Namaste," she intones menacingly.

Lorelei tells us about the children she passed this morning on her way to the studio, two boys who sat on the sidewalk pouring a cup of water into an old Snapple bottle and back into the cup, over and over, all the while getting soaked with rain. "Kids have so much to teach us about present moment awareness," she says, and I realize that the distance between parents and non-parents is as wide as the parking lot at the King of Prussia Mall. Lorelei reminds us to savor the moment, no matter how wet and uncomfortable, to find the extraordinary in the ordinary, like children do without any effort. But all I can think of is their mother, who was probably pissed they were playing with garbage, yelled at them for getting wet, and had to be running late.

"Do you remember when mud was fun for you?" our teacher asks us.

I suppress my impulse to explain that mud is fun to anyone who doesn't have to mop it up and do laundry. That when you have no place to be, who cares what the kids are up to? Plus, if you think about it, kids are generally short, close to the ground where they can pay more attention to things like mud, strewn bottles and garbage. But what they do not possess is an ever-increasing sense of time passing, time we don't want to spend cleaning up after them because we'd rather leaf through a fashion magazine that makes us feel like shit for being a size ten. So we teach it to them, drum it into their tiny skulls. *We're running late!* we chant at them, and *Hurry up for God's sake! Don't make a mess! Take off your shoes!*— our own desperate mantra, one I've blindly embraced and handed down to my kids so they can grow up to run grim-faced through the rain toward some dry, antiseptic future. *Great,* I think. *I've already ruined them.*

"So today, let this be your intention: when you find yourself in the rain, struggling with a challenging, uncomfortable pose, just stay there, in the mud, *where the lotus grows.* Breathe into the discomfort, into the challenge, and allow yourself to get sopping, soaking wet."

And then we're off. Cat and cow. Sun salutations. Et cetera.

Exhale.

My new neighbor's triangle pose is flawless, exultant.

Inhale.

I can't stop staring.

Exhale.

Her butt is as tight as an Olympic sprinter's and those sinewy arms—graceful as a ballerina's. She's got flat abs, slender ankles… Even her toes are beautiful. Her blond hair, pulled in a messy bun, looks camera ready. The thin gold chain around her neck glitters. How lazily it traverses her trapezius as if it had been art-directed to look just so. *Fuck her,* I think. Then, *Om shanti.*

Exhale.

And then, wonder of wonders, when it's time to practice handstands, while the rest of us battle it out with the walls, our wrists and weak core muscles, guess who nails it like Nadia Comaneci in the middle of the room, in slow motion no less, putting even Lorelei to shame. That's right, my new neighbor. And you can bet the cellulite on your flabby ass that she gets a round of applause. Mine is not as rousing as the others, but my hands do clap together more than three times. More to show everyone that I can handle her brilliance without falling to pieces.

Maybe my petty jealousy is why, toward the end of class when we're winding down, bridge pose is a spiky bitch and reclining twists leave me feeling like my spine is filled with wire. And with the rain, even corpse pose feels like a backbend. I never thought I'd feel so old at forty-one.

Exhale.

Exhale.

Exhale.

My sister snores, overworked ER nurse that she is, and I feel a jolt of maternal tenderness toward her that did not exist before I had children. I listen for my beautiful neighbor but can't hear her because she's perfect. Her shavasana is perfect. She's probably actually dead. I can barely lay on my back, it hurts so much. By the time I relent and stuff a meditation cushion under my knees, the brass chime sounds for us to rouse. I wiggle my fingers and toes as instructed even though I'm wide awake, turn onto my side in the fetal position. I rise into a fragile lotus position, breathe into the pain, and bow to the great teacher who dwells within me with great effort and strain.

On our way out the door I overhear my new neighbor quizzing Lorelei on her credentials.

"Yes, but did you ever actually study in India?" she asks, insistent, holding her rolled-up mat between her knees as she reties her hair.

For the first time in the two years I've known her, Lorelei looks ruffled. Pissed.

Jeannie and I glance at each other and head out. On the sidewalk I tell her that the fresh piece of yoga meat is the one building the McChateau next door.

"Come on," Jeannie says, frowning. "That's just wrong. You gonna leave a flaming bag of dog shit at her front door?"

"I think she's married to her contractor. They were flirting and kissing in her driveway this morning. But it was weird."

"Weird how?"

"Who flirts with his own wife?"

"I have no idea."

I rub my spine.

"Look baby, I can see how much pain you're in. Go home. Take a Motrin. Masturbate. Call a doctor."

"I will," I lie. I never call doctors. I'm into damage denial.

"Then give the bitch a bag of dog shit."

Chapter 3

Sleeping late is no longer an option with the racket next door. The slate roof tiles are being nailed in one at a time. Thankfully, however, the copper drainpipes are in, as is the new stone facing, painstakingly installed brick by elongated pastel brick, and quarried locally according to my new neighbor—whose name, Neil learns one afternoon while dragging the recycling bins from the curb, is Anna Lisko.

"Why locally, because they're environmentalists?" I say.

We're sitting at the kitchen table sipping coffee, still in our pajamas. Well, Neil and I are wearing various ancient pajama bottoms with sweatshirts. Chloe's wearing actual PJs, printed with tiny red owls. Outside our window the neighbor's house looms, stony and menacing.

"Mommy's a tiny bit jealous of the new neighbors," says Neil to Chloe, who's making a card to welcome our neighbors, all her idea. I beam at her as if I had anything to do with this rare burst of generosity. "Perfectly understandable," he adds.

"I'm not jealous," I say. "I think it's ridiculous."

"What's jealous?" Chloe says.

"Jealous is when you want what someone else has," I say.

"Why are you jealous, Mommy?" Chloe asks.

"I'm not jealous," I protest again.

"She likes their locally quarried stone, for one thing." Neil takes a gulp of his coffee.

Chloe says, "I'm jealous of Tess at school." "She has real feathers stuck to her hair. They're so beautiful."

"Feathers, huh? We have some feathers in the basement. Want me to glue them to your head?" Neil says, taking her for a ride.

"No!" Chloe says.

"Anyway, it's hip to be green," Neil says to me.

"Daddy, you're not *green!*" Chloe says.

"It's hip to be obscenely wealthy," I say to Neil. To Chloe I say, "Green means caring about the environment," but she's already tuned us out. I turn back to Neil. "What else did she say?"

"Eve, I can't remember. I'm so tired. Can we talk about it after I've slept?"

"I didn't realize this was so tiring for you," I say.

"She said they were going for rustic modern," he says. "Okay?"

I purse my lips with disdain. At him. At the neighbors.

"Try not to let it get to you," Neil says, reading my expression.

"I just don't get it," I say. "Why didn't they just buy a mansion in Bryn Mawr? Put us all out of our misery. It's not as if the houses on our street are that small, you know?" That chunk of change Neil made off the Fat Ass song, plus what we got for our apartment in Brooklyn, afforded us a far nicer house than we ever could have gotten on the salary he makes now. Up until now our house felt palatial, with its ample living and dining rooms, eat-in kitchen, family room add-on, screened-in side porch and four generously proportioned bedrooms. Plus there's the finished basement rec-room and three-and-a-half bathrooms. I had no idea there was so much room for improvement.

"I wish they had bought in Bryn Mawr," Neil says. "Then I'd get some freaking sleep." He yawns again. "But—oh yeah. That's the other thing she said—this is their pet project."

"Pet project? What would constitute a big project? Installing a moat and drawbridge?"

Neil shakes his head and takes his mug into the kitchen for a refill. "Eve, I didn't ask."

"What kind of spy are you?" I ask.

"Daddy's not a spy, Mommy. He's a word processor," Chloe says.

"Word processing *manager*, honey. Big difference," Neil clarifies.

Sam races into the kitchen. "Dad? Mom? Have you seen my Bionicle? The one with the white body and blue claws? *Not* the one with the blue body and black arms."

"So was she nice at least?" I ask, digging.

"Have you seen my Bionicle?" Sam asks again, louder.

"Why? You going to befriend her now? The evil renovator?" Neil says, sipping his fresh cup of coffee.

"I thought I might," I say, scratching a piece of hardened egg yolk from the table.

"Mommy," Chloe says, chastising me like a mini-puritan. "Stop being jealous."

"Mom! Dad!" Sam cries. "I'm talking to you!"

"She was very nice," Neil says.

"Hmph," I say.

"WHERE IS MY BIONICLE?" shouts Sam.

"Sam would you relax for two seconds? Daddy and I are trying to have a conversation!" I shout. Then, "Do you think she's pretty?"

"Here we go," Neil says.

My husband's dalliance notwithstanding, you can probably tell by now that I'm not graceful when it comes to women who are thinner, prettier and richer than me. My mother used to hate watching me suffer, because I was her youngest, and because she felt guilty for marrying yet another dud. Growing up, whenever I was jealous of a girl at school, she'd reason that the girl's personal life had to suck. My mom would surmise that her parents' marriage was in the toilet, and she probably made poor grades. But, if she made good grades it was because her parents pushed her too hard and didn't allow the girl any autonomy. If she excelled in sports or art or music, it was because she bought into an empty and shallow culture that my mother had transcended lifetimes ago. *That poor kid*, she'd say, believing her own fiction. They couldn't win, those pretty popular girls, being judged by my mother.

By the time my mom was finished undermining their academic successes, social status and good looks, I didn't pity them like I was being coaxed to. I pitied myself for not shining brightly enough to be threatening. I longed for someone to tear me apart so I could know I was worth something, but all my mom ever did was tell me how amazing I was, for simply tying my own rainbow-striped shoelaces, pouring my own milk into a bowl of Sugar Corn Pops. I never believed her compliments.

It wasn't until I had kids that she started treating me like shit and I could breathe. I think she tears me down now because I'm a better mom than she was. That, and I've managed to stay married to my original husband for more years than her three marriages combined—almost fifteen. Maybe given the circumstances, it's nothing to brag about, but the kids at least enjoy a lulling continuity.

My mom still practices her method of dismantling the perceived competition. She believes her bullshit, that she can erase her own anxiety, build herself a soft-walled citadel of victory over all her adversaries. Her strategy is obviously flawed, well intentioned as it is. Because there are plenty of people out there who simply have it all, whether or not they are society's evil drones. And I bet Anna is one of them, living so handily next door.

"She's smoking hot and you know it," I say to my philandering husband.

"Eve, we have to get past this," he whispers.

"You think this is easy for me?" I whisper back.

To Sam, Neil says, "Come on, buddy. Let's go find your Bionicle."

They leave and Chloe holds up her drawing. She's drawn each stone and colored them in varying shades of purple and gray. "What's that brownish square right there?" I ask her, wiping my eyes which have started to tear, pointing at a speck in the corner of the picture.

"That's our house," she says, grinning like a person whose neural pathway for keeping up with the Joneses has not yet been forged.

Chapter 4

I knock on the door, solid walnut, distressed just so. Perfectly rustic-modern. The handle alone looks like it cost five hundred dollars. A minute later Anna Lisko is standing before me, in faded cut-offs and a tank-top, barefoot and glowing as if she's been sandblasted by her construction crew. She looks thirty-five, going on sixteen.

"Hi! I'm your new neighbor? I'm Eve? Myer? We met at yoga the other day?" Can I stop talking like I'm asking questions? Please? I try not to stare at her tight little thighs. I hand her the housewarming basket that I spent an hour assembling—getting the cheese, crackers and wine to lie just so on a swirl of raffia. I added the card Chloe drew, wrapped the whole thing in cellophane, and tied it off with enough curling ribbon to reach the Schuylkill River.

"Oh sure," she says. "Anna Lisko. Nice to meet you." She takes the basket with a delicate hand, turning it this way and that, inspecting. "If only we ate gluten," she says, forcing an air of wistfulness.

I nod and smile as she looks at me, and it's way too long that we're standing there so I do what I do in times of social crisis: I gush. "You have a beautiful practice," I say. I am not going to dismantle this bitch's successes and natural gifts. I am going to bask in their heady glow, and be happy for her.

Anna beams. "That class was sweet," she says, as if reminiscing about a toddler's birthday party. "I studied under Pattabhi Jois," she explains. "In Mysore."

"Wow," I say.

"I saw you were having some trouble with wheel pose. I could help you with that," she says. "I do a little instructing."

"Oh that's not necessary," I say, my body going rigid.

"Come in," she prods. "I'm certified Jivamukti."

I stammer a protest but she's so stunning I find that my feet are already over the threshold.

I'd been in this house once before, to give the old owner a plateful of nearly homemade Christmas cookies—sliced-and-baked and slightly burnt. I remember the house was perfectly acceptable, other than being carpeted in mottled navy worsted nylon. The space I see before me now, despite the stacks of cardboard boxes, is magazine-ready—wide-plank floors, airy rooms that open into one another. Light cascades from skylights in the brand new cathedral ceiling above, and a balcony hallway leads to what I suppose are bedrooms. The furniture is all low-slung, clean lines. Cashmere throws. Gold Buddha statue already situated in a corner.

"Do you work?" Anna says, her voice echoing from the kitchen where she sets the basket on a honed marble countertop.

"Next year I'll start looking," I say, following her. "Chloe's only in half day kindergarten, so." The guilt begins to gnaw at me for not working, but with my fine arts degree the only thing I'm qualified for at this point is retail or waitressing—either one of which will give me hives of anxiety caused by irate customers, dealing with a manager who would surely be younger than me by at least a decade and therefore sadistic and filled with idealism, or waiting on Those Main Line Women, with their rhinoplasties and North Face puffer jackets, who will openly pity me as they walk out the door trailing clouds of Tocca perfume and bouquets of thick, glossy shopping bags.

"I envy you," Anna goes on. "I wish I could spend more time with Deepak."

"Chopra?"

"Dorian."

"Oh," I nod. "Sorry." Meanwhile this just compounds my guilt. I'd had it all figured out in my head—Anna was the spoiled house-wife who spent her days shopping and lunching while her husband toiled away eighty hours a week in some law firm. "So what do you do?" I ask.

"I coach," she says.

"What?" I ask. "Football?" It just pops out. I know she doesn't really.

"I coach *Life*," she says, a flicker of hostility darkening her lovely features. "Primrose Enterprises, LLC. It takes up *so much* time, being a small business owner." There's a handcrafted decora-tive bowl on the coffee table filled with her business cards, nestled in among small crystals. She runs over, plucks one out and hands it to me, along with a complimentary stone.

"Thanks," I say, inspecting the rough purpley crystal and set-ting it on the counter.

"Lilac Lepidolite. It helps with stress. I can see your aura."

"Are people still reading auras? I—I don't mean that in a bad way. I just thought that it was more about meditation, choosing a Hindu god, buying the little statue, eating local seasonal biody-namic fermented cabbage…"

"Your aura is in trouble, Eve. It's broken at the edges, especially around your third eye and root chakra. Red jasper might help with that. You could really use a crystal clinic. And yes, crystals and auras are still *in*." She pairs a hostile set of bunny quotes around the word *in,* to show me what an idiot I am.

"Sorry, I just—I'm not much of a believer."

Anna points at a spot above my head. "Yes, I can see that." Then she picks up the purple stone, leans over and rests her elbows on the counter. She turns the stone in her fingers, making it sparkle in the streaming sunlight. "This one contains lithium. Very calming." She slides the stone back toward me. "I'm actually kind of famous for my chakra healing kits," she admits, swiping a coy finger across the counter.

"I'll have to broaden my horizons," I say, pocketing the rock and studying her pale pink business card. "Maybe no one's ever presented it the right way before." I figure I will be living next door to this maniac for God knows how long. I'd better be civil.

"Do you cook?" I ask, nudging the subject to safe territory, indicating the eight-burner industrial stove.

"I *love* to cook," Anna says, grasping her ankle and standing in a casual tree pose. "I'm a bit of a foodie," she adds, apologizing. "Terrible in restaurants. Waiters *hate* me. I always have to know exactly what's in my food. Do you know there are places that still use MSG?" She is affronted by this piece of news.

"I can barely find the time to reheat," I say, smiling at my own joke.

Anna says, "I don't even have a microwave," as if she's just performed a magic trick.

I barrel on: "When do you do it? You must be so busy, with your coaching." I'm angling for her to fess up the maid, the butler, the nanny, the personal trainer.

"Here, lie down," she says, changing the subject.

"Right here?" I ask. We're standing in the kitchen. "I'm not really dressed for yoga."

"You're fine," she coos, eyeing my long twill shorts and oversized T-shirt. "Lay down."

"Don't I need a mat?" I ask.

"The floor is cork," she says, hopping up and down, demonstrating its buoyancy. "I can heat it if you like."

"Oh sure, why not," I say, slipping off my flip-flops and lowering myself to her burnished, dustless floor as she flips a switch near the huge farmhouse sink. I may as well take advantage of her luxe offerings.

"Can you get into a bridge pose without a problem?" Anna asks, kneeling beside me. I can see that she has no cellulite, not even in the crease where her thighs squish against her calves when she squats. Already I can feel the heat under me.

I'm not an invalid, I think. But when I lift my butt off the floor, a spasm of pain shoots through my spine and I drop to the floor with a small bounce.

"Wow, you're really hurting," she says, gripping her knees and staring at me until I feel a thousand years old.

"I'm fine," I groan, and allow her to help me up.

Anna abandons her little impromptu healing project and makes us a pot of Japanese twig tea. She sets a tray down on the coffee table and pours us two tiny cups out of a black teapot with a woven straw handle. The sofa is so long and deep I'm not sure how to sit on it, so I just perch on the edge, rubbing my spine and noticing the gigantic blood-colored ceramic lamps dwarfing me, as large and bulbous as a lumberjack's beer gut.

Anna sits in lotus position on the floor, her torso as straight and tall as a flagpole. "I know a great acupuncturist," she sing-songs, her eyes mischievous.

"Oh, that's okay," I say, swatting her suggestion away. I can only give so much.

"All pain is a blessing," she intones. "It invites us to heal."

Then I am as blessed as they come, I think.

She gives me puppy eyes, the little flirt.

"I'll think about it," I say, hoping this will end the conversation.

Anna leaps up and jetés out of the room.

"It's feeling a little better!" I call after her, wondering how my mother would tear her apart. She'd call her flashy. Tacky. Shallow.

When Anna returns a few moments later she's waving another business card. She flops down next to me, closer than before. I can smell her all-natural shampoo and essential oils. She hands me the card, panting excitedly. Such a confident, sexy creature.

Billy Dorian—Eastern Healer in the Western World. Acupressure. Acupuncture. Alternative Modalities. TRUE HEALING. Then it gives a phone number and an address in Mount Airy. No website. No e-mail, which I find interesting. Mysterious. Old school.

"Read the back," Anna instructs and I turn the card over. It has a quote, printed in a font meant to evoke the far east: *The soft overcomes the hard. The slow overcomes the fast. Let your workings remain a mystery. Just show people the results. ~The Tao*

"Thanks," I say and pocket the card, not intending to use it, and starting to feel like the unwitting spectator of a live infomercial.

"Isn't that intense?" she says, entreating me with her smile to agree.

"Do you know this guy?" I say.

Anna nods furiously. "Billy's my husband."

"And he does contracting too?" I say, confused.

"He's not a contractor," she says, tilting her head, squinting at me.

A moment of silence where we stare at each other quizzically, frozen in time and space. Then the flicker of recognition. A flurry of flustered faces. My nerves jangle. My heart pounds in my throat. We speak at the same time. I say, "I must have seen him working around the house. No big deal. Tell me about the acupuncture."

She says, "He does a lot of work around the house. Maybe you saw him the other day. He's been doing all sorts of stuff."

We laugh and look warmly into each other's eyes. *See?* My mother would say. *Her marriage is a wreck!*

"—But healing-wise, he is a *genius*," Anna says. "I made him put that quote on the back. I am telling you, Eve, if you go to him, he will *heal* you. *And* he will heal things about you that you didn't even know *needed* healing. He is a true master. Ugh. I cannot say enough good things about him."

I pull out the card again, inspect it. "He works in Mount Airy? Why not here?" I ask.

"He refuses to move his office. He loves that old house. It's practically falling apart." Anna looks at the floor. I'd swear she was ashamed. Beyond her flushed face stands a black and white wedding photograph on a rough-hewn shelving unit. It's the only displayed anything in the house. In the picture bride and groom stand ankle deep in the sea, their backs toward the camera, facing two different points on the horizon. She holds the corner of her dress. Her long hair whips in the wind. His dress pants are rolled to his knees.

"Beautiful picture," I say, noting that the groom is not much taller than Anna. Proof that the man who kissed her in the driveway is not her husband.

Anna turns and appreciates it. "Deepak loves that photograph for some reason. Insisted we put it up. Isn't that funny? Took me two hours to find the box it was in." Her head whips back around to face me. "Oh Lord, I have about a million calls to make."

The Mercedes pulls into the driveway as Anna stands, plucking a few more crystals from the bowl on the coffee table. "Take these," she says, glancing toward the kitchen. "On the house. They really work." She carefully transfers the stones from her hand to mine. "This one will bring you great happiness," she says, pointing at a clear one. "Herkimer diamond."

"What do I do with them?"

"Relax. Breathe. Lay them on the corresponding chakras."

I nod, wishing I could ask her, *so who exactly were you kissing in the driveway?*

Soon little Deepak comes running in wearing mini Uggs, followed by the nanny, an older Hispanic woman weighed down with Whole Foods reusable totebags. "Hello," she says to me, her eyes flicking up and down my body as she sweats and strains and finally sets the bags down. I have a sudden urge to help her unpack and realize that I identify with the nanny more than I do with Anna.

I introduce myself, hold out my hand to shake. The nanny doesn't take my hand, but pats her chest and says simply, "Julie." Julie begins unloading groceries—bottles of kombucha-chia seed tea, packages of exotic flours, fresh meats, Illy espresso and produce galore—while Deepak runs over to a truck on the floor.

Anna intercepts and twirls him in a circle like she's playing the part of a mother for a mortgage loan brochure. "Hello my darling," she says, but Deepak presses his hand to Anna's face and pushes her away.

"Not now, Mommy. I busy."

Anna looks at me, embarrassed, and I joke, "Oh I have no idea what that's like." She looks horrified, so I say, "Oh my God, I'm kidding. My kids treat me like shit all the time."

"Really?" she asks, her face alight with hope. "I thought it was me. That he's picking up a vibe about my damage."

"Damage?" I ask, intrigued.

"Well, you know, all the horrible things about yourself that you secretly think make up the real you—kids sniff it out like bloodhounds. Anyway, I get a little nervous about it, and that feeds his distaste and it cycles viciously. And Julie—well. She just doesn't operate on that plane. Deepak adores her. I guess I should be grateful, huh?"

I cannot for the life of me imagine Anna Lisko as a person who suffers from any lack of self-esteem. She strikes me as nothing but an object of envy for thousands of self-doubting, cellulitey women, whether or not she's cheating on her husband with the contractor.

"Mommy, stop talking," Deepak says, pushing his truck around the floor.

"See what I mean?" Anna whispers to me.

"Your mommy's explaining all sorts of interesting things to me," I say. Then I crouch down and look the little boy in the eyes. He is a beauty, with golden ringlets and huge liquid brown eyes, olive-toned skin that glows rosy just under the surface, so soft I feel invited to stroke his cheek with a thumb.

He looks at me, waiting and wary.

I hold out my hand. "I'm Eve," I say. "Nice to meet you."

Deepak looks at my hand.

"Now you hold out your hand," I say.

Thankfully, he does.

"Now we hold hands and shake."

And so we do. He cracks an embarrassed smile.

"It was nice meeting you," I say. "Now you say, nice meeting you too."

Deepak giggles and says, "Nice meeting you too," in a goofy voice. I stand up.

"You're so good with kids," Anna says, impressed. I catch Julie looking at me from the kitchen, over Anna's shoulder.

"Only with other people's," I say. Then I whisper, "Mine are assholes."

Anna laughs charitably, not sure what to make of me. I get that a lot. Am I snarky? Sarcastic? Pessimistic? Just a plain old bitch? It could go any way.

"Anyway, thanks for the chat," I say, marveling to realize that I like this woman. She's not one of Those Main Line Women after all. She's—what? Keepin' it real? Showing her soft spot? There's something vulnerable about her. Something I can relate to without feeling intimidated or blinded by her razzle-dazzle. "And all this great chakra crystal stuff. It was really nice meeting you," I make my way to the door.

Deepak looks over at us and says, "Shake hands!"

Anna and I smile sheepishly and clasp hands for the boy, and I feel a slight jolt as if it's the dead of winter and she's just slid toward me across a carpet. A flash of a memory—or a vision—shoots through me. Something watery. *Dead Sea,* I think for some reason. She grips my hand and a face floats to the surface. Anna's face. Dead. I shiver.

"Shit," she says, tilting her chin to the ceiling, and releases me. I swear her eyes are welling up with tears.

"Are you okay?" I say. "Wait. What did you—"

"It's nothing," she whispers, holding her hands up as if I've got a gun pointing at her forehead.

"How did you *do* that?" I ask, whisper back, matching her tone, yet not sure why. "And why are we whispering?" I add.

"Do you have any dolphin CDs?" she says suddenly, completely ignoring my questions.

"Dolphins?" I stage whisper. "What are you talking about dolphins for?"

"Eve," Anna whispers, stern this time. She grasps my hand again. Another image comes to me. My face. My mouth. Duct tape.

"Oh my fucking God, lady. I get it. But Jesus."

"One second." She sprints out of the room again, leaving me standing in the doorway, a bevy of befuddlement fogging the edges of what was, until now, my reality. Julie's still in the kitchen, stirring something in a bowl, her back to me. Does she know? Can Anna send everyone messages? How does her husband deal? Or that contractor? Do they know? Does Deepak?

By the time Anna returns, I am fully and thoroughly freaked out. She presses a CD into my palm. I turn it over. *Dolphin Serenade,* it reads. *Magical Marine Melodies to Mend the Mind, Boost the Body and Soothe the Soul.*

"Um, thank you?" I say, forcing a smile, peering into her eyes to see if I can discern the joke. Is she serious with this crap?

"So beneficial," she intones, placing her hands on her hips, all traces of weird witchiness gone. I am desperate for her to take my hand again but I can tell she's through with her demonstration.

Meanwhile, there is no way in hell I am even going to open this thing.

"Don't knock it till you try it," she says, commenting on my transparency. "And thank you for the gift basket."

"Sure," I say, waiting for her to explain, wishing she would tell me how she transported images into my brain. *Please*, I plead silently.

"Another time," she says and I'm about to say thank you when I realize that she's just answered my unspoken question. Which means she can read my thoughts too. Does this mean she can read everyone's thoughts? Wait—does Anna know that I know that she's cheating on her—of course she does. *She knows all.*

"You are freaking me out," I whisper, remembering the duct tape image.

Anna smiles warmly.

Does she know all the horrible things I've been thinking about her? All my jealousies? How can she even stand me?

"I've heard much worse," she says. "You're an honest woman, Eve. Angry and sad and confused, but far less than I usually encounter. Please don't worry yourself over this." She leans closer. "And keep your mouth shut. We can talk about it some other time."

"Got it," I say, grimacing. Maybe I don't need to know any more for now. Maybe it's far too revealing. And way too unsettling.

"You got that right," Anna says, and ushers me out the door.

Chapter 5

hey're having a get-together, out on the brand new patio. I try to sleep at two a.m., well after Neil was supposed to have returned home, but the music and noise inhibit this plan. Every time I doze off, a woman goes, "Aaaaaahhh haaaaaaaaaaaaah!" like some deranged dodo bird.

The fact that I am not cackling along with them begins to gnaw at me like gas pains. I want to be there, to party with Anna, to find out more. I feel like I'm in an M. Night Shyamalan movie. It's kind of awesome, in a surreal way, and kind of they'll-put-me-away-for-life-if-they-knew-I-believed-my-neighbor-was-telepathic. Which is why when I had Neil on the phone earlier, I opened my mouth to tell him and then clamped it shut again. He already thinks I'm crazy enough.

I pick up a Post-It and scribble, ~~Smart, angry, sad and confused~~ *Feisty and innovative heroine goes on tour with magical telepathic neighbor. Wows audiences around the globe—Vaudevillian style—with powers of mind-reading and telepathy. The two become the toast of the town, partying with the likes of the Rockefellers.* Sticking the square of yellow paper to the wall—my first period piece—I know just what I need: my binoculars.

My lenses roam the patio through the darkened bedroom window. Everyone sits gaily sipping drinks and laughing, and then I see why Neil never returned home from work to eat snacks and watch a Netflixed episode of *Weeds* with his wife. It wasn't that he was mugged and killed, since he failed to call—he's next door partying, swilling a beer, laughing heartily over some shared joke with Anna, who's wearing a fluttery blood-orange sun dress that shows off her everything. I swear I can see him leering at her breasts. Is she reading his mind right now? Would she tell me if she were? Oh my God, the possibilities! I suddenly burn with a desire to be her number one confidante. Her go-to chum. Her one and only BFF.

I wrench the binoculars away and run downstairs after checking on the kids to make sure they're dead to the world. Then I open the back door and stop myself on the deck. What am I wearing? Raggy culottes, an old threadbare cotton tank top, no bra, bare feet. I have no makeup on and my hair is tied back in a greasy ponytail. I'd be foolish to run upstairs and start primping for a party I'm not even invited to. I remain staring, paralyzed, until Anna turns and catches my eye. She gestures broadly for me to come over. Neil sees me too and echoes her sweeping arm motion, which is a terrible, horrible thing because I look like shit.

I advance across the lawn, impersonating someone who's perfectly happy wearing nearly transparent rags, smile as easily as I can muster and accept the first drink offered my way, by Anna—a Coors Light. Is this supposed to be ironic? Neil kisses me on the cheek and then excuses himself to go "hit the head." Classy. And already drunk. I frown at him as he disappears into the McChateau.

"Eve! I'm so glad you came over," Anna says, tipsy, overcompensating. "How are you *feeling*?"

"What do you mean?" I ask, paranoid already that she's been reading my mind from her house. Or is it like a cordless phone? Her powers stop working once you're at least five hundred feet away?

"You pretty much nailed it," she says, nodding, impressed.

"So you don't know that I want to whisk you away to rule the world?" I ask.

"I like you, Eve. You make it so easy. I've never met anyone so honest," she says.

I peer at her sideways.

"I mean it, Eve," she says.

"I like you too Anna," I say, looking at the rectangular flagstone beneath my bare feet, certain I'm blushing.

Anna smoothes her dress as if we've just emerged from a dark bedroom together. "Oh hey, did you get a chance to listen to the CD?"

"It's so relaxing," I lie.

She says, knowing I'm full of shit, "Please listen to it, Eve. It will really help to heal you."

I nod, and try not to wince. I can't believe a woman with such stunning attributes would seriously listen to that shit. Maybe the privileged are more enigmatic than I know.

Anna and I share an awkward silence. "Oh, there are some fabulous seaweed snacks over there," she says, pointing at an L-shaped stainless steel grill console. "They're amazing with the beer."

"Oh cool," I lie again, and head over.

I dump my Coors Light into the recycler and reach for a bottle of white wine, a New Zealand Chardonnay. Dry as a bone.

"Want me to open that for you?" a voice beside me says, and I turn to see a man who is so cinematically handsome that I nearly lose my balance standing still on a warm, breezeless evening. My eyes trip over his body, milking every detail despite my better judgment—the pursed petal lips and steely blue eyes, the rocket-straight eyebrows and sharp cheekbones. The broad, perfectly proportioned physique under a faded maroon hoodie, worn without anything underneath, unzipped to the sternum; the long rumpled shorts topping a pair of beat-up old motorcycle boots. It's like he just rolled out of bed, on the set of an Oliver Stone movie.

"Sure, thanks," I say, and hand him the wine, offering him a quick smile.

"Billy Dorian," he says, placing the bottle on the console. We shake hands, firm and tight, heat zooming from my fingertips straight into the pit of my stomach and up to my head where it short-circuits my rational brain.

Now, I don't mean to be dramatic. I've only just met the man, but I am cursed with an affliction and I know when it's been triggered. I've felt this before upon setting eyes on a beautiful man—well, beautiful *boy*. First comes the jolt of electricity, followed by the wasted months of stuporous obsession, culminating in suicidal despair where I sequester myself to the bedroom floor with a blanket, a pillow and Jeff Buckley on the iPod. It's my most pathetic trait, far worse than my jealousy of rich, thin, stylish women, more terrible than my exasperation with Neil or my irritability with Sam and Chloe. No. My infatuations are The Worst. They shame me.

So it scares me, the buzzing in my body—tits, heart, crotch—as I watch Billy conquer the wine bottle with one of those pneumonic gadgets that must come with a novella of instructions. Unkempt honey-tipped spirals explode from his head, complementing his slight mustache and beard the way a down quilt complements a king-sized bed on a blizzardy Sunday morning. Cozy. Inviting. Post-coital.

His elbow brushes against my breast and I feel a tingle that cascades along the insides of my cheeks, causing me to drool. I shake it off, ball my hands into fists.

Neil never consumed me, not even at the beginning. I knew from the start that I wouldn't disappear into a man like Neil. He made me laugh, sang Mariah Carey songs to me, and most importantly, he called when he said he would. He was "into me," like the good book said he should be. So when he asked, I said Yes.

But now, under the weight of kids and past transgressions, a failing economy and suburban sprawl, our marriage is leaking like the Titanic. I need a hot neighbor like that boat needed an iceberg. Of course I could say the same thing about Anna and Neil, the way he's drooling over her. Add telepathy to the mix and we have ourselves a Situation. And yet, there's a part of me that always yearned for a type of love that could sail across the heavens like a comet.

"Eve Myer. I live right there," I say, pointing at my humble abode. I keep my gaze trained on the patio stone like an oppressed Afghani woman.

"Oh yes. Eve. I recognize you from the cracked aura."

I smooth a palm over my hair as if this will repair my aura just as I realize that Billy is fucking with me because he is grinning.

"Wow, you guys talk about everything, huh," I say.

"Anna likes to share," he explains diplomatically.

"Young love," I say, with an air of authority. It's something I've gained in my fourth decade—the ability, at the very least, to take pride in my breadth of experience.

"Why, how long've you been married?" he says, pouring us each a glass.

"Fourteen years. You?"

"Just one. I guess you win."

"So I guess that makes Deepak..."

"It's a long story," Billy says.

I know enough not to pry, even though I'd love to, especially since the kid actually looks like Billy. I say, "It took me until last year to realize that Neil does not give a shit about ninety percent of what I say. It's a bitter pill, but we're both so much happier now." I paste a smile to my face for that last bit. I am not going to let this beautiful man get under my skin, especially not when his wife probably already knows from across the patio. But she's got to be used to it. I bet every woman he meets falls at his feet. Well, it won't be me. I've lived too damn long. Crushes are lipstick lies. Glittery mirages of happily-ever-afters that do not and never did exist except in Disney fairy tales and Julia Roberts movies. And Meg Ryan movies. And—okay—Renee Zellweger movies. Plus, I'm nothing like Neil. I keep it between my ears and allow nothing between my legs. That counts for A LOT.

"Can you tell Anna that?" Billy says, holding out his glass to cheers me.

"Awkward," I say, clinking my glass against his. "Plus, she can read my aura. It's already a mess. I don't want to trash it completely."

"Oh yeah. The aura. It always gets you in the end. *She sees all.*" He waves his fingers and widens his eyes, demonstrating new age wack.

"You don't buy it?" I ask, surprised at his pessimism, when he's married to a bonafide witch.

"Personally? No. But a hell of a lot of women around here do." He tucks a clump of hair behind his ear, which is perfectly shaped. Excellent lobe. Not swingy, not too attached. Baby-bear just right.

"So she's a shyster," I goad. "How does she sleep at night?" *Does he not believe in his wife's abilities? How could this be?*

"I think in some way we're all shysters."

I smile at his cynicism, allowing myself three seconds to stare at this Roman coin. One. My eyes flicker from his motorcycle boots to the shadow inside his hoodie. Two. I can just discern the top of a six-pack beneath his exposed, hairless, well-muscled chest. Three. I have to stop myself from shaking my head and exclaiming, *Are you for fucking real, man? Are you KIDDING me?*

"But, and um," he says, "I'm slightly drunk, and, we just got into a fight."

"That sounds serious," I say, thinking, *a fight? Oooh... What about? Tell me EVERYTHING.* I lift my gaze for a peek at his face. I swear I've seen him in an Armani ad. On a billboard in his Calvins. Something somewhere.

"It's nothing new," he says, sipping. Then, "Good wine." He's changing the subject.

"It's pretty amazing," I say, glancing at his hips, and take another calming swallow.

"Anyway, I'm sorry to dump my petty marital troubles on you. I hope you don't judge me negatively."

"Not at all," I say, gesturing with my half-empty glass. "Totally understandable."

He turns to face me fully, as if seeing me for the first time. "Cool neighborhood," he concludes and I can feel myself blush because I know he means me, that I'm cool. And I haven't felt cool for over a decade. If this living breathing work of art turns out to actually be nice—interested in what I have to say—there's only one thing for me to do. Pretend he doesn't exist.

Still, I say, fighting a losing battle, "There's always a second chance to make a first impression." We clink glasses again and drink, peering at each other and fighting smiles. Then my balding, paunchy, adulterous, weasel of a husband makes his way toward us, following Anna like one of those stray dogs you meet on budget Caribbean vacations. I suddenly envy Jeannie for being divorced.

Anna's neckline is so droopy I can see smudges of white skin where the sun never reaches, on the inner edges of her breasts. Freckles scatter across her chest and collarbones. Her gold chain glints in the twinkle lights. Her teeth are impossibly straight and white.

I smile at her and ask silently, *does your ridiculously attractive husband even know about you?*

"Billy, this is Eve!" Anna squeals. Then she squeezes my arm, owning me and slightly shaking her head. *Is this her answer? Billy doesn't know?*

She turns to Billy. "I told Eve she *has* to make an appointment with you. She has *horrible* back pain."

"Sure, I'd love to take a look," he says, biting his lower lip. He knows that I know that he already knows this, since Anna tells him everything. But she doesn't *show* him everything. It's been two minutes and I already have an inside joke with Billy and the inside scoop with Anna.

"Sounds great," I say, hoping I sound blasé. I drain my glass and Billy refills it.

"Neil tells me you're a writer," Billy says, as Anna excuses herself to mingle, giving my arm one last squeeze which catapults the image of Billy on a beach, standing ankle-deep in the water and making out with a woman—me! Whoa, what the hell is that supposed to mean?

Neil looks at me, as if awaiting my permission to follow Anna. I shrug, stuck in my telepathic puzzle, and off he goes, fresh beer in hand.

"What sort of stuff do you write?" Billy asks, tugging me back to earth and to his unearthly beauty.

"I'm just messing around," I say, feeling my face flush. "I didn't know Neil took it seriously."

"I was asking him about you," he says. "We were talking about passion. How when you're a kid you do whatever you want, and how hard that can be as an adult, especially once you have kids, and a mortgage, and health insurance... And Neil said that you managed to stoke the creative flame."

"Did he mention that the laundry's piled up to the ceiling?" I ask, inferring Neil's resentment but also finding myself thrilled by the fact that Billy was asking about me.

"I always wanted to write a book," Billy says. "But I got involved in this racket." He gestures to the house with his fresh glass of wine.

"You must like it, though. I mean, who sets out to be an acupuncturist?"

"Someone who was helped by it and doesn't know what else to do, because he's too ADD to focus on writing a book." So now he's not only beautiful and interested in what I have to say, but he's flawed and envious of my life. The tables have officially turned.

"Are you really ADD?"

"Probably."

"What'd you need acupuncture for?"

"I had an accident a while back."

He's being cryptic, I think. Most people would drool at the chance to divulge a personal tragedy. "Is that what you'd write about?" I say.

"Partly," he says, and when I indicate for him to expound he turns the conversation back to me. "So tell me about one thing you've written. Please?" he says, and I see that he has secrets of his own. And that he's charming as hell.

"Just ideas for now," I say, wondering if I'm lucky or unlucky to have inherited this strange, beautiful family next door. "Weird stuff." Equally cryptic. What am I going to tell him, that I jot down sadistic suburban goth? Actually, that doesn't sound so bad. "It's Kafka-esque," I explain, stealing a page from the literati.

"Kafka-esque? Sounds interesting," Billy says. "You ever share it?"

"I haven't yet," I say, peering at him, wondering if I have what it takes not to finger myself to this man's image. A hand slaps Billy on the back as I chastise myself for even considering a masturbatory fantasy, especially in front of Anna. Billy turns and says, "Ah, here he is, man of the hour! C'mere, you."

Anna follows the man of the hour—a very tall man wearing a chunky gold watch—into our little powwow, grasping him by the upper arm. She studies his toothy profile, almost reverent, and takes a sip of her Coors. Neil arrives on her smooth bare heels.

"Eve, Neil, *this* is the asshole who's responsible for all the noise. My brother Rick, contractor extraordinaire. Didn't he do a great job?" Billy kneads his brother's shoulders and I choke on my sip of wine. I glance at Billy to see if I can figure out what the hell is going on, then grab Neil's hand and pull him toward me, wishing I could whisper in his ear.

"What are you doing?" he says, losing his balance and glancing at Anna to make sure she didn't see and doesn't disapprove.

I glare at him. "Forget it," I hiss, and he gives me the wide-eyed shrug—the *whad-I-do-this-time* shuffle.

Rick, besides standing a head taller than Billy, is more groomed—like a show dog—with a waxy, varnished complexion and wiry close-cropped yellow hair. Neil and Rick shake hands. Then I do. His grip is moist but strong. *Rhodesian Ridgeback*, I think. Billy introduces Rick's wife, Beth. She stands with us, smiling and nodding along with the conversation, her face as broad and open as a wheat field, until she laughs at something Neil says and lets out that horrible screeching laugh. Her shoes tell me that she and Anna have only Rick in common—red patent-leather ballet flats with gold medallions. They seem off, like when tomboys wear prom dresses.

"You did a great job," I say to Rick, being extra nice because something very messed up is happening. Rick is like a stretched out faded version of Billy—a bad Xerox—the kind you wouldn't get charged for at the township library.

Rick can't stop talking about how each stone was custom fitted, how they planed and stained and even chained salvaged barn wood for the living room shelves and mantel, how he wouldn't be surprised if Main Line Weekly came by to do a spread on the place. I could swear Billy's eyes glaze over.

"As soon as we win the lottery, we'll hire you too. Make ours bigger than yours!" Neil says and Beth cackles again. My husband looks at Anna to see if she dug his joke but she's glistening in Rick's direction. I turn to Billy and he looks at me, apologetic, as if he understands completely the drudgery of a long marriage.

"I am the only contractor in the entire county who insulates with recycled denim," he tells us, showing a mouthful of large crowded teeth. He grabs Billy around the shoulder and says, "There's nothing I wouldn't do for this guy." *Like fuck his wife?* I think, glancing at Billy, who's grimacing.

Anna shoots me a glare then, and I feel slapped. Chastened. *Sorry*, I think to her, and she nods.

I finish the last of my wine and grab Neil's hand in a curious display of ownership—as if he is the last island of normalcy—as we are ushered inside by Rick for a grand, exhaustive tour covering every square inch of the *pet project.*

When we step across the heated kitchen floor, Anna takes me by the arm and whispers in my ear, "I wish I could talk to you more. I'd like to explain. Can you have coffee tomorrow?"

"Sure," I say, as we enter the master bedroom.

I have to clamp my mouth shut so my jaw does not land on the silk carpet. Our entire first floor could fit in here. Rick shows us the remote controlled blackout curtains, even in the walk-in closet— to protect the clothes from sun damage. Intricately carved wooden valances top each elongated window. "From a neoclassical palace just outside Kolkata," Rick says, pointing. Then he fingers the top layer of the elaborate window treatments—yards of silk that shimmer iridescently as they puddle onto the floor. The king-sized bed is outfitted in a patterned jewel-toned bedspread that looks as if it took twenty virgin seamstresses a decade to complete. The entire ceiling is draped in silk, so that the room resembles a sultan's tent. A dazzling hot pink chandelier hangs from the nucleus, dripping in crystals. I can't imagine Billy choosing any of this on his own. When I sneak a glance at him, he's rubbing a hand over his lips and looking at the floor as if all this could go away if he wished hard enough. Even the doorways have been custom carved into scalloped arches, to honor the architecture of Anna's appropriated motherland.

Deepak's room is almost as large as his parents' room, with a custom-built loft bed designed to resemble a cruise ship, replete

with portholes, a deck and a railing. I shake my head slowly, wondering how long it will be until he wearies of his nautical theme
and starts angling for an equally expensive redesign—a medieval
castle, seventies disco, Mir Space Station...

Then we're touring the family room, with its jumbo flat
screen mounted to an exposed brick wall. We're invited to sit at
the mahogany bar salvaged from an old English pub stocked full
with top-shelf booze, while Rick regales us with stories about each
architectural detail. A handful of leather wing chairs upholstered in
Union Jack-patterned leather surround a gray flannel poker table. I
wonder who plays cards. Maybe Rick and Beth when they come to
visit? A fleet of sumptuous chaises covered in orange mohair velvet
beckon me to come and nap and a pair of sixties Lucite bubble
chairs hang suspended from the ceiling. Sam and Chloe would pee
their pants over those things. Each retro kitschy piece was pro-
cured by Rick and Anna on a trip to London. How convenient.

As the acid yellow flokati rug massages my toes, I feel a tug on
my hand. I turn to see Deepak looking up at me. I glance at Anna,
who seems to be listening intently to something Rick is explaining
about the lighting, which he demonstrates from command control—an iPad-like remote he holds in one huge palm. I can only see
the tips of Billy's boots peeking out from behind a fat column in the
middle of the room, and as the lights dim and brighten in varying
rainbow shades, Deepak tugs me toward a door behind the bar. I
look around the room once more, and then we're gone.

"Where we going, hombre?" I ask as he takes me down a hallway lined with wide-plank floors, walls the color of tea-stained
muslin and smoky gray-painted mouldings. He stops at a door,
turns and says, "Vamanos."

I obey, out of curiosity mostly. And because he's so frigging cute.
But this feels all sorts of wrong. Because where is Julie? And why
isn't this preschooler sleeping? And what does he want with me?

Inside the plain white room is a gold embroidered cushion on the bare floor. There are no shelves, no furniture, not even any decorative trim. The one deep-set window is dressed simply with a loosely woven linen panel tacked to the wall above. The room is monastic compared to the rest of the house—compared to the rest of the country, really—and I have the feeling it's more Billy's style.

Deepak points at the cushion. "Siéntate."

"Si," I say and sit. I think that's what he means. Deepak arranges my legs in the lotus position.

"Shake hands," he says and I smile as we shake, pride bubbling through me that I had an effect on this boy. Then he takes my index fingers, touches them to my thumbs, places them on my thighs. "Close you eyes," he instructs.

This is insane. "Deepak, what are we doing? Don't you think your mommy is going to wonder where you are?"

"It's okay," he says in a slightly Spanish accent learned from where, Julie? "Her knows where I am."

"She does?"

"Her always knows."

"Okay," I say. "And can she see your aura?"

"Of course," he says.

"Can you see my aura?" I venture, my eyes still closed.

"No. Only mama sees," he says.

"Does your daddy see?" I ask, even though I know he doesn't.

"Silencio," he says, and sits in front of me on the floor, mirroring my posture. I know this because I peek. When I clamp my eyes shut again I hear, Ommmmmm, so I take a breath and join the young mystic. What else is there to do?

The door opens and I whip around to see that Rick has popped his head inside.

"Okay if we join you?" he says and Deepak opens his eyes wide. Then he leaps up and bolts out of the room through his uncle's long legs. Rick grimaces at me. "I wanted to show everyone the walls in here," he explains, ignoring the child who's just run away as if terrorized. Then he walks over to the window and pats the thick wall. "You know, the whole Wales farmhouse vibe we got going over here. These walls are *eighteen* inches thick."

"Huh," I say, glancing at the door, and before I have a chance to think things through, I'm on my way out the door. "I'll be right back!" I call over my shoulder as I retrace my steps down the hallway, through the Anglo-fanatical family room where everyone seems to be taking turns with the lighting console, through the obscenely industrial kitchen, airy living room and finally out the rustic-modern front door, where I see Deepak on the lawn, heading into the street just as a pair of headlights speeds his way. "Deepak!" I scream, running into the street and grabbing him just as a seafoam green Range Rover barrels past, nearly smashing the boy. Tears spring from my eyes as I clutch him to me. I whirl around and there's Julie reaching out for him, finally available, her face crisscrossed with pain. Deepak lifts his head from my shoulder and lunges into her arms. Julie murmurs Spanish into his ear and strokes his hair while the boy shudders with sobs.

Neil and Anna are there next. Neil continues staring at Anna, who runs up to her son and strokes his back but he squirms away from her and Anna flinches as if he'd just kicked her in the stomach. She stares as Deepak burrows deeper into his nanny's embrace, Anna's own arms hanging useless by her sides.

Billy arrives, pulls Anna into a hug and looks at me tentatively over her shoulder. I can't tell if he's blaming me for what happened or thanking me with those fierce eyes. Neil plops down on the grass and takes deep breaths between his knees. "Everyone okay?" he croaks, holding his head. Rick and Beth show up last and survey the scene from a safe distance. Beth takes his hand and kisses it, and I could swear she smiles.

Chapter 6

The next morning I go to see if Deepak's okay. Really I want to see if Anna's okay. Watching her stand there, so impotent with her own kid, cracked something open inside me—something positive and communal that could prevent me from fearing her and fantasizing about her husband. I'm standing in the front entryway, having been instructed to wait by Julie, when Billy appears, in an old T-shirt that clings to his torso, and Adidas track pants. Seeing him jars me again in all my body's hot spots. I have to gain control over this. It's just physiology, I tell myself. He's just a combination of perfectly proportioned curves and angles. It's just math. Fibonacci's golden ratio. A jumble of colors, pheromones, textures. Soft… Hard…*Ugh. Someone hand me a vibrator already.*

I force myself to find a flaw on him, but there are none to be seen. Even his fingers are perfectly proportioned. Not too thick or stubby. Not womanly. Perfect manly-yet-graceful hands that probably know exactly how to please a woman. *Neil is the love of my life,* I chant, and think of my depressed, adulterous, overweight prince charming.

Billy shoves his hands into his pockets and I tell myself to knock it off but his pants sag an inch, revealing a flat ribbon of belly above a hint of dark hair that I should not be noticing, let alone enjoying. I swallow and meet his eyes. "Morning," I say, then look away.

"Hey Eve," Billy says, as if we've known each other longer than twelve hours. "Thanks again for last night. If you hadn't been there…" He trails off.

Though appeased by his approval, I avert my gaze. Study the texture of the walls. Smooth. Smooth texture. Plaster. Paint. Fascinating. "No, of course," I say to the wall. "I can't imagine." I shake my head, then imagine Deepak getting smacked by a Range Rover. I stifle a shudder. I should never have let him lead me into that thick-walled little room stolen from the Welsh countryside.

"Yeah," he says, as if we envisioned the wreckage together, and he toes an invisible piece of lint on the floor with a bare foot.

"How's he doing?" I ask, returning my gaze to the wall.

"He's fine. He's in the tub right now splashing away like nothing happened."

"Kids are good that way," I say. Then, "What about Anna?"

"Anna's sleeping," he says, which seems like code for, she's sleeping it *off*. "But I know she'll be glad you came."

"Oh, sure," I say. "Let her know I asked for her, and if she wants to come over for coffee—or anything—but she mentioned coffee last night at the, uh…" I trail off and turn for the door because I really need to be going. Now.

"Wait. Don't go just yet," Billy says, and I turn back toward him, hopeful and kicking myself for it. I should not be this attracted to a guy, let alone my new friend's husband who lives right next door. I'm hitting middle age. I've got two kids. Been married forever, to that fucking schmuck. My life is a done deal, a closed door. I may as well stick my head in the oven.

Billy says, "I'd like to take a look at you if you don't mind."

"You what?" I nearly screech, my heart leaping like a skittish terrier.

Billy smiles. "Your back," he says, his eyes twinkling. "Anna told me how much pain you're in. And after last night, I'd imagine it might be worse. You know, from the stress of saving a kid's life."

"Oh," I say, and my heart settles back into its cavity. My face, however, ignites. He might not be able to see inside my head, but he's got to know what I'm thinking.

Without another word, he leads me to the guest room. Tatami mats and a red lacquered ceiling evoke a Japanese tea house. The walls are papered in gold, a burnished sky against which calligraphied cherry trees forest the room. An antique kimono graces one wall, skewered in place with a stick of bamboo. I look at the platform bed in the center of the room, upon which lies an oversized coverlet that origamis onto the mats in precise triangles. I stand there, waiting to be instructed. Am I going to be lying down? With Billy hovering over me?

As I ponder my fate he positions himself behind me. I can feel his heat as his fingers connect with my spine, tracing the bones from the small of my back to the nape of my neck. I barely turn my head, nearly paralyzed. I just allow the touch.

"Touch your toes," he says. I can feel his breath on my ear.

I bend over.

"Slight scoliosis," he says softly, reading my vertebrae like braille dots.

"Stand up again," he instructs and his fingers trace my spine again. "Lordosis," he says, and then prods the tight muscles on either side of my lumbar spine, causing me to wince in pain and catch my breath.

We stand there in silence for a few moments longer, Billy's hands roaming my spine, my hips, ribs and neck, while my heart thunders despite my best efforts to be cool.

"You're a hot mess," he finally pronounces happily, coming around to face me.

I want to say, light as air, *You could tell all that from my spine?* But I can't joke. I can't even speak. So I just stand there while he smiles.

"Think about coming to see me at the office," he says. "I'm pretty sure I can salvage you."

The first thing I do when I get home is Google Lordosis. Commonly known as swayback. "Oh my God," I say, slamming my laptop shut, sprinting over to Neil and yanking up my tank-top. "Do I look deformed?" I ask him.

Neil's still in bed, wearing striped pajama pants and a T-shirt that reads, *Dead Inside.* Since I don't hear the kids I assume they must be in the basement watching TV.

"Billy told me I have swayback." I turn left and right in front of the mirrored closet doors, trying to locate my horrible disfigurement.

"When did he do this?" Neil asks, his eyes glued to an old issue of the *New Yorker.*

"Just now. He uh, gave me a, um, free consultation."

"Oh he did, did he." Neil peers at me over the top of the magazine.

"He kind of insisted," I explain. Which is not a lie.

"You don't have swayback," he says, casting off the idea like it's a stray hair clinging to his shirt.

"It's not like I'm making it up." I run into the bathroom and grab my hand mirror, race back to the bedroom.

"Well, it looks fine from here. Completely normal. Sexy even."

"Ugh, would you stop." I point out how the curve is misplaced. "Do you see? Do you see how it should be lower? I looked this up."

"I don't know, Eve. I'm trying to relax."

"If you stand up we can compare. I can show you," I say, peering over my shoulder into the hand mirror.

"What did I just say?" he scolds.

"Do you want to see my scoliosis? He said I have that too. This is an *abomination.*"

"If it'll make you happy," he sighs, giving in. He slaps his magazine across his lap.

I walk around to his side of the bed so he can get a good look. His fingers lazily swipe the bones of my vertebrae. "Yep, there it is," he says.

I remember this one morning years ago, way before kids and his little weekend getaway. Neil and I were on the subway on our way to work. I told him I felt sick and he said, *Sure you do, Eve.* I told him I felt dizzy. He shook his head and rolled his eyes. I told him everything was going black and he nodded like I'd just asked him for a stick of gum. The next thing we knew I was slumped on the floor, being pulled to my feet by passengers who'd rushed in to save me, my husband jockeying for position behind their concerned faces. Afterwards, I sat with my head between my knees getting my back rubbed by a stranger. My husband kneeled before me and apologized for not taking me seriously. I was elated.

"Don't you care?" I ask. "I am *grotesque.*"

"You are not grotesque." He picks up his magazine.

I stomp into the bathroom and scrub my teeth, glaring at my reflection. I spit and rinse, then sit on the bed. "Who the hell does he think he is?" I say, marshaling my rage. *Who is this beautiful man to diagnose me with such horrible disfigurations?*

"He's a guy who needs to make a living to pay for a very expensive house," he says, flipping a page.

A half hour later, we're in the kitchen nursing coffees. The kids are still in the basement with the TV going. I'm still wondering how all of these horrible ailments came to be associated with my spine as

I thumb through *eat pray love* for the third time. Neil's traded his magazine for a two-inch thick biography of Chairman Mao.

"Something weird is going on with the neighbors," I say, glancing at the hairline fracture in the wall behind Neil's head. I swear that thing was not there a week ago.

"The neighbors are fine," he says.

"I saw Rick kiss Anna."

"Don't go making accusations. You barely know these people."

"I know who's married to who."

"Eve, do you think we can please just not go there with these people? It's none of our business. We're all doing the best we can."

"Convenient philosophy," I tell him.

Neil grumbles something about good intentions.

I skim a few paragraphs and my jaw stiffens. "Who the fuck is Elizabeth Gilbert to get *paid* to travel to Italy, India and Bali to find herself after a *breakup*? Are there not more deserving people on this planet?"

"You mean like you?" Neil suggests.

I glare at the man. "I mean, I identify with her *bourgeois suffering*—the search for contentment, self-actualization, enlightenment, but come on. Why her?" I say.

Neil puts his book down and sighs. "Anything else?" he says, his tolerance hanging on by the fingernails.

"No. I'm done, thank you." I turn my book over on the table and rub my eyes. Now would be about the worst time to tell him that Anna is a mind reader. But what about Jeannie? I could tell my sister, surely.

Meanwhile, Jeannie would say that rereading *eat pray love* is yet another of the ways I torture myself—by throwing myself across jealousy's merciless train tracks. *You really think it's a good idea to read that again when it makes you so crazy? You really think it's a good idea to obsess about the neighbors?* Then she'd light into me for not forgiving Neil once and for all—since he is the man I chose not once but twice—and getting on with my life. And she'd rip the book—or the binoculars—from my hands and give me something soothing, like *Radical Acceptance,* a well-loved and oft-highlighted self-help tome from her vast collection. *You need to find peace with what IS,* she'd implore, holding my face in her Russian immigrant hands.

I toss my book aside and scan the shelves behind me for something less inciting—maybe an Austen novel would cleanse my reading palate. "Anyway, did you have fun last night?" I say, which is really code for *tell me how you really feel about Anna Lisko.*

"They're a nice family," he says. "It'll be good for us to hang out with some new people." This, I take to mean, *I will be spending as much time as I can next door, soaking up the effervescent company of Anna Lisko.*

"You don't think they're a little, I don't know, too dazzling?" I say, compelled to goad.

"They're fortunate. Nothing wrong with that," he says.

A vine of loneliness tendrils from my belly button, anchoring me to the old oak chair. "My back really has been bothering me," I say. Which means, *Love me, God dammit.*

"Maybe Billy can help you," he says. Then he gets up to refill his mug—the one with the cartoon of a fat guy sitting on the toilet with a cup in his hand and the caption—*Coffee gets you going!* I bought it for him the year we started dating. It's still his favorite.

In my chair I work my fingers over my spine, feeling for the disloyal vertebrae, pretending my fingers belong to someone else—someone who is crazy about me.

Chapter 7

﹏◖ ᷅ ◗﹏

As I maneuver the minivan through the streets of Mount Airy I see that the leaves are already turning on some of the trees, lending the air a sunburnt glow. It took me three weeks to make the decision. In those three weeks I watched from my window as Billy and Anna played with Deepak in their yard, as Julie drove back and forth from Whole Foods to the house, always with the boy, as Billy came and went in his vintage Jeep Wagoneer, as Rick visited during Billy's absences, pulling to the curb in his gleaming red pick-up truck. I watched from my window, through her window, as Rick teased Anna with playful slaps and kisses. Not once did I see Anna and Billy kiss. I suppose that shouldn't have surprised me, but it did.

As for coffee, it never happened. Every time I thought about taking up Anna on her invitation to talk some more, my feet just wouldn't cooperate. I came up with excuses not to go, primarily because she knew, especially when I was in close proximity, what I was thinking about—fantasizing about—which was Billy. It started to feel like a bad sex event, where you fuck the wrong guy for desperate reasons and the only way to move on is to pretend it never happened and that the guy doesn't exist. And I started to doubt my affection for her, and slowly reverted back to feeling resentful and afflicted by her visual perfection.

And then Neil started helping Anna in her garden, and their time together looked so intimate that I couldn't bring myself to join them. I watched as they planted tulip bulbs, my husband brushing her arm with his own, accidentally on purpose—pathetically obvious. Another morning he helped her haul soil in a wheelbarrow and after that he gifted her with some of his own treasured compost. But when he brought her a cup of coffee, handed her the mug with the cartoon man on it, I decided I could not wait a moment longer to do something about my aching back.

Some streets have the curb appeal of a discarded Gatorade bottle—monotonous rows of boxy brick twins. Then I turn a corner and am greeted with a collection of stately stone houses with A-frame rooftops and old-growth trees. Finally I find the street. The houses are Victorian behemoths, grand and dilapidated, shadowed by ancient ivy-covered maples. Low iron fences lean every which way, bracketing overgrown wildernesses, keeping no one out. The house I'm looking for is the largest, with mullioned bay windows and black trim. Through the narrow iron rails of the one fence on the block that stands at attention, explosions of sea grass spill onto the sidewalk. The front entrance is lined with Russian sage, echinacea and sea oats. I take a narrow brick path to the side door, bypassing a wraparound porch where a black lab dozes beside a rocking chair.

Inside I perch on an old velvet sofa and stare into the dead eyes of a twelve-point buck trophy hanging above the marble fireplace. This room, with its somber olive tones, is not about humor or whimsy or putting frightened patients at ease. I imagine a stretching rack waiting for me in the examining room. Something iron and medieval, with chains and spikes and dried blood. I have perhaps just made a huge mistake, biting Billy's bait, coming here like this. My back barely hurts today.

Three huge paintings glow softly under individual brass light fixtures, each one thick with glopped-on paint, abstract and imposing. Great arcing swirls and drips of red and black hint at the idea of a glorious, muscular destruction. In the center of the seating arrangement a coffee table is strewn not with magazines but with carefully examined books—*Autobiography of a Yogi. Lame Deer, Seeker of Visions. The Bhagavad Gita.* The faint smell of burnt sage kisses my nostrils. I look at the door. Stand to leave, then see a copy of the Tao on the table and slump back into my seat.

I open to a random page.

If you want to become whole,
let yourself be partial.
If you want to become straight,
let yourself be crooked.
If you want to become full,
let yourself be empty.
If you want to be reborn,
let yourself die.
If you want to be given everything,
give everything up.

Crooked, I think. *Let myself be crooked.*

"I love that one," he says, standing over me, pointing at the passage.

I yelp. Turn beet red. "I had no idea you were there," I say, clutching my chest.

"There's a door," he says, amused, pointing behind the sofa at a bare expanse of wall.

"Huh," I say, squinting, not seeing it. Must be hidden.

"Glad you could come, Eve." He pats me on the shoulder, lets his hand linger there for a moment. I shiver, despite the warm temperature.

In his cargo pants and thermal top, you'd never know you were in the presence of a doctor—a healer. Whatever he is. He turns and I see he's wearing a string of prayer beads around his neck. Behind the beads he's got another accessory—a whitish shimmering Nike symbol of a scar that begins somewhere under his shirt on the right and traverses the nape of his neck, disappearing into his hair behind his left ear. I wonder if he prays on those beads. If there is more evidence of his misfortune beneath the cover of his clothes.

In the examining room, the rear wall of the house has been replaced with floor-to-ceiling windows, framed in industrial steel. Beyond this transparent layer an exterior privacy wall covered in cascading vines and flowers secrets us away. A waterfall descends through the foliage, its burbling captured and filtered through a sound system inside. Thankfully, there's no medieval torture device but rather a staid looking padded examining table in the center of the room. An old desk stands in the corner upon which is placed a silver Apple laptop. A transparent exercise ball waits beside it.

Billy gestures for me to sit on the examining table, just like a real doctor would. Then he walks over to his desk and types something into his computer. I study his profile—his scars, the bridge of his nose, the swell of his deltoid, flat belly, graceful stance, how his pants hit the perfect spot on his hips.

He looks up from the screen and catches me staring. "You know I don't take insurance, right?" He says after a silence, the beginning of a smile teasing his lips.

"I was thinking you didn't," I say, averting my gaze to the floor. It was a mistake to come here. I should leave right away.

"What tipped you off?"

"The deer heads," I say. "Obviously."

Billy laughs then. "You want to know how much I charge?" He asks, his eyes turning back to the computer.

"No," I say. I should pick up my bag and hightail it back to the burbs.

He walks over to me. "Lie back," he says, and pats the examining table.

I obey, my heart thundering in my ears.

"Lift your butt," he says.

Balancing his own butt on the exercise ball he slides his hands underneath me and quickly finds a tender spot along the ridge of my pelvis on the left. My breath catches as much from the pain as from his solicitous touch. This is more than I bargained for. I pictured flirty banter, but this—this is intimate. I let my lower half ease into the cradle of his hand, surrendering.

"Does that hurt?"

"Not too much," I say, my breath knotted.

"That's the spot," he says with unconcealed enthusiasm, and moves his fingers to palpate the right side, which does not hurt nearly as badly. As he explores the terrain of my lumbar he asks questions about the origins and quality of the pain. I tell him it's been off and on for years, at times debilitating but mostly a corseted sensation of immobility that hinders my yoga practice—especially backbends. He stands up and the exercise ball rolls away. He leans over me and grips the protrusions of my hips, pressing one side into the table and then the other. "The right side is really open," he says, more to himself than to me. "When does it feel the worst?" he asks.

"When I wake up," I gasp, trying not to be dazed by his pummeling, gripping hands.

"Any other times?"

"After yoga," I admit, praying he doesn't squeeze a fart out of me.

"And when does it feel the best?"

"In my sleep."

"The pain started a long time ago..." he says as if mind-reading my anatomy, walking around the table to examine my other side. "...twenty years ago probably. Is that when you met your husband?"

"Yeah. How did you know?"

"Just had a feeling."

I look at him, the way his hair halos his face as he leans over me. "Is that bad that my pain started when I met Neil? Because it sounds really bad."

"Oh no, it's nothing like that. It's more of a shift. Life changes outside us create body changes inside. Nothing to judge positively or negatively."

Right, I think.

Billy licks his lips. "Yeah," he says, crossing his arms in front of his chest and regarding me like a vintage Volkswagen. "I think we can save you."

The way his mouth moves when he speaks, how the breadth of his chest and shoulders pulls at his shirt, watching him move across the room—languid, graceful, feline—all of it plants a hot seed of desire in my gut. "Yay," I say and grip the edges of the examining table. The tissue paper crinkles.

Another hour passes like a minute, as his hands discover all my tense points. I close my eyes before our time is over and think, this is the best two hours I have spent in months. Much too soon he tells me to sit up and says, "That'll be nine hundred dollars."

Chapter 8

I still don't think you saw what you think you saw," Neil says on Sunday night. He's sitting at the kitchen table with his guitar, working out a new song while the kids sleep mercifully hard upstairs.

"Are you telling me that from Billy's driveway to our kitchen window I can't discern him from his gargantuan brother? Why don't you stand right here, look out the window and judge for yourself?" I'm at the counter cutting sandwiches into squares— natural peanut butter, sugar-free jam, sprouted multi-grain bread. I lay down my knife, wipe my hands on an oily dish towel and head for the door.

"Eve, please don't go into the driveway," Neil says. "I don't need the CSI version. Maybe you saw what you say you saw. I just don't want to believe it. They're nice people."

"You're so smitten with her," I say, looking around for a scrap of paper. I have another idea.

"I am not," he says, but he can't keep a straight face.

I look up from the pile of school papers on the counter and glare at him.

"What?" he asks, trying not to laugh.

I shake my head. "Typical," I say, picking up an old fundraising flyer.

"You have nothing to worry about," he says, but his laughter escapes. Nervous weasel.

I take a pen from the can Chloe decorated with construction paper and sequins and scribble on the back of the flyer—*Midlife crisis throws suburban dad into drooling tailspin over newly arrived gorgeous neighbor. Wife watches and plots revenge as affair, disguised as shared love of gardening, unfolds. Serpents and poisonous apples figure heavily. Think: Biblical Eden meets Terminator 2.*

I am through with Anna Lisko. She and Neil can have each other. The bitch didn't even wave to me when she pulled out of her driveway this morning. I know she saw me standing there in the front yard. I was hauling the recycling to the curb and she just— snubbed me. All that talk about what an honest, smart woman I am, and wanting to talk. What a crock of shit.

"Eve, I know you don't believe me, but you can trust me," Neil says, working hard to straighten his face. "Believe me, I learned my lesson."

"You are so... ugh." I squint at him, then read over what I've written.

"What? What am I so?"

"I don't know," I say, folding the paper in quarters and pocketing it while trying to get a glimpse into the neighbors' windows. Their curtains are drawn. "It's like you're done with the whole— issue—so I should be done with it too. It's like you think I need a kick in the ass to catch up to you, when you're the one who needs to catch up to where I am in all this. And where I am is still trying to move on," I say. "And it's not easy. And it takes time. And I'd appreciate it if you could respect that."

"Why are you always looking at their house?" Neil says, strumming a moody chord.

"Don't change the subject," I say, heading back into the kitchen and unrolling a sheet of foil.

"I just don't know how else to prove to you that I'm sorry—that *nothing* like that will ever happen again," he says. "You know that was an anomaly. You said it yourself."

"I was trying to be fair."

"What about now?"

"I don't know," I say, wrapping the sandwiches, stowing the foil back in its drawer and slamming it shut with my hip. "Look. Off the subject, there is one thing I need to tell you."

"You mean my girlfriend cheating on her husband with her brother-in-law isn't enough?"

"Please don't be flippant about this." I say.

"I'm sorry. What do you need to tell me?"

I grab a Tupperware container of sliced apples from the refrigerator. Divide it into a pair of natural unbleached waxed baggies from Whole Foods. "I saw Billy Dorian today. Went to his office. He examined me. Says I could use a few months of treatment. Says he can, uh, salvage me."

"Oh and *I'm* smitten?" he says, now vindicated.

"I have *chronic* back pain," I say, defensive.

"You've had back pain for four years. You never went to get it checked out before."

"*You* told me to see him," I say. "And I told you it's been bothering me." I'm about to add another point but then realize I already sound like I'm justifying. And yet he's the one with the adulterous record.

Neil stares at me.

Now it's my turn to laugh nervously. "It's true!" I say, giggling.

"How much," he says.

"Nine hundred, but I told him—"

"Nine hundred dollars? Eve, are you smoking crack?"

"I told him there was no way. I paid him fifty for the one session—"

"Fifty dollars for an hour?"

"He spent *two* hours with me."

"What, like special treatment?" Neil asks, slightly alarmed.

"Not at all," I say, far too enthusiastically. And I wonder, did he give me a free hour? "But he says he's going to come up with something that will work for both of us," I say.

Neil says nothing. Just stands his guitar on end, holding it by the neck.

I stuff the sandwiches and apples into a pair of insulated lunch totes along with individually wrapped cheese sticks, and tubes of pink yogurt.

He says, "It's not that I don't want you to get better."

"It just sucks that my back pain now qualifies as a luxury item," I say.

"I know. I'm sorry. I just can't stand all the spending."

"But I'm barely buying anything!" I cry. Neil can attest to this. It used to be I couldn't log onto Amazon without buying at least twenty-five dollars worth of stuff just to get the free shipping.

"I know. That's what's so disturbing. It's like we're leaking money and I don't even know what to do about it. I barely make anything as it is."

"Who knows," I say. "Maybe one day I can sell some of my writing."

"That would be great," he says, but I can tell by the tone of his voice that he thinks I'm deluded.

Chapter 9

I can't afford nine hundred," I say the following week, entering the spooky waiting room where Billy is sitting reading the Tao. "It's not going to work."

He responds with a short passage: "*Free from desire, you realize the mystery. Caught in desire, you see only the manifestations. Yet mystery and manifestations arise from the same source. This source is called darkness...*"

"Does that mean we can work something out?"

"I have an idea," he says. "I just have to sort it out. Do you think you can pay half, in monthly installments and agree to be my guinea pig without knowing what the experiment is?"

"That sounds irresponsible and reckless," I say, not calculating the monthly bill. And I am through feeling guilty about a simple set of doctor's visits. I am not doing anything wrong. I am working on myself. My healing. I am being responsible to my health and thereby my children and even Neil. "I'm in," I say.

"Good," he says and holds out his hand. We shake, and I burst into a smile.

"You're happy today. Used to getting your way?" he says.

I certainly can't tell him I'm smiling because I can't not smile around him. His very visage sparks an engine inside me that's been laying dormant and dusty for years. And I cannot tell him that I saw him and Anna arguing last night through my window, and that I saw him drive away like a bat out of Hell, and that the fact of it made my adolescent heart sing with sinister hope, despite my efforts not to be drawn to him. "Are you used to getting your way?" I ask.

"You first," he says.

"Almost never," I say. "You?"

"Not much," he says, which I find surprising, given his magnetic appeal. His lower lashes alone. His lips. The hollow under his cheekbone. Even the stubble on his throat seems haughty with self-satisfaction.

"So what's up with the deer heads?" I ask, puncturing the silence that follows. Next time, I think, looking at the creepy paintings, I'll ask him about the creepy paintings.

"I'll tell you all about the deer heads, but first tell me how you're feeling." Billy leads me into his office. He leans against his desk and crosses his arms in front of his chest, peering at me from those intense blue eyes. His hair is so messy it looks like he just rolled out of bed.

I perch on the edge of the exam table. "A little better," I say, knowing that the difference in my pain is so subtle it wouldn't be worth mentioning to anyone else.

"How so?"

"Well I wasn't as stiff when I woke up this morning," I say, which is true.

He nods. "So. You want to know about the deer trophies?"

"I do," I say.

"Bow-hunting," he says. "Soon they'll get company. You eat venison?"

"I'm mostly vegetarian," I say. "Trying anyway." I picture Billy crouching silently in the woods, aiming at a giant buck from behind a sleek crossbow.

"Trying?"

"I had a little salmon over the weekend."

"How was it?"

"Anti-inflammatory," I deadpan.

He lifts his eyebrows. "That's good. I like a client who is her own advocate."

I try not to beam from the compliment. "Actually it was really fucking good. Surprisingly good. And it was the frozen kind from Trader Joe's. Still butt-expensive, every so often we splurge. Is it okay that I just said fucking?"

Billy holds up two fingers. "You said it twice. *Fucking.* There. Three times. Most auspicious."

He gestures for me to lie down with a sweeping palm. "Do you think your body has its own intelligence?" He asks, cupping my heels one at a time, slipping off my leather ankle boots and placing them on the floor. Then he wraps his hands around my waist, presses his fingers into my back.

"Uh, yeah," I say, hating how much I enjoy his hands on my body.

"I wrestled in college," he says. "Before I dropped out of school."

"You dropped out?" I say, my voice rising with gusto.

"Don't sound so excited," he says.

"Why'd you do it?"

"Same reason most people do I guess. I couldn't see the point."

"But you're a doctor."

"I'm a *healer.*"

"Did you go to medical school?"

"I studied with shamans."

"Shamans?" I ask, my curiosity throbbing along with the rest of me.

"I'll tell you all about it sometime." Billy begins to prod my abdomen, pressing the tips of his fingers deep into my muscles until I wince.

"What are you doing?" I ask, trying not to gasp.

"I like to get in there on the opposing side. Break up the fascia. Reset the front and the back follows."

"Huh," I say, not understanding a thing but knowing I'll agree to anything he proposes.

"So anyway, after I left school I went from bad to worse and wound up in the hospital."

"How?"

"Motorcycle accident."

Ah, the boots, I think. *And the scars.* "This is what led to the acupuncture?" I say, picturing Billy as a college dropout laying in a hospital bed wearing a thin blue gown, dependent on other people for his health, vulnerable, angry, his world in tatters, his leg in a sling, head taped shut.

"Sort of," he says. Then sheepishly admits, "I had some uh, anger issues."

"Oh," I say, chastened by his candor.

Billy goes on. "I got in a fight this one night. Nothing unusual. And after we were both good and bloodied I rode off. To clear my head, get away." He pauses, remembering. "And the bike just slipped out from under me. We skidded across the highway—it was late thank God, so the highway was empty. Anyway we went careening. I shattered my leg. The only good choice I'd made that day was to wear my helmet. Otherwise my head would have been chopped meat."

"Jesus," I say. "I'm sorry. I'm *so* sorry."

"Yeah," he says.

"Do you share this story with all your patients?" I venture, unable to resist quenching my thirst for every piece of information.

"Only a special few," he says, narrowing his eyes at me.

"I see," I say, and stop myself from asking who the others are. I'm not sure I want to know.

"So once they released me," he says, "I said screw it. I flew to China and lived with a healer."

"Wow," I say.

"Yeah. And so one thing that happened was, my body was craving meat. The way yours is maybe. I wasn't getting enough nourishment. My body knew, even if my mind had all these *ideas.*" He says the word like it's a menace. "My teacher said *Billy, your body smart but your mind so dumb. Stop listening up here and start listening here.*" He gestures at his head and then pats my belly.

"That is so intense," I say. "But how do you go from a hospital bed to living with a healer in China?" My life, as much as I've wished for it to be, has never demonstrated a penchant for the magical, except in my imagination. But Billy's life strikes me as part magic at least.

"My mother had a picture of a beautiful mountainous place. She kept it in her bedroom, taped to the side of her night table. It might have been from *Life Magazine.* I don't know. It was foggy and lush, with palm trees, a river cutting through the center. A valley with a town, nestled right in there. The mountains reminded me of something from a Dr. Seuss book. They were unreal."

"Can't you ask her about it?"

"She's dead."

"I'm sorry."

"It's okay. She's been gone for a while. I was just three when she—" He stops talking.

"That must have been hard. I'm sorry—"

"No, no. It's okay. Really. I barely remember her."

"How did she—is it okay if I—" I start.

Billy sighs. Slumps where he's sitting on his exercise ball. "Is it okay if we save that story for another time?" he asks.

"Oh my God, yes, I am so sorry. I just. I get so. I'm just. Curious. I'm sorry."

"No worries," he says, then takes a breath. "So anyway, Julie told me that the place in the picture was Yangshuo, that there were healers there, that my mother had always wanted to go. So I figured, why not start there?"

"Did you take it as a sign?" *How did your mother die?*

"I guess. I was confused. Grasping. You know how it can be like that?"

"I do," I say, thinking of every morning when I open my eyes and feel in a deep recess somewhere in my soul that there is something else—something more—waiting out there for me, if I only knew where to look.

"Not that grasping is any good. But for this chapter of my life, it was as good a move as remaining where I was."

"Which was?"

"With my brother," he says.

"Oh." I'm about to ask about his dad but Billy's face clouds over and I get the distinct feeling that now would not be a good time to press forward with my interrogation.

"Anyway, when I got back to the states, I started a pretty intense meditation practice in the Taoist tradition, and learned pretty quickly that in Chinese medicine, and basically every traditional culture on the planet, people eat animal products. They revere the animals they eat. They worship them. They're not mindless about it, you know?"

"Cave drawings," I say slowly, realizing he's making total sense.

"Exactly. You never see a cave drawing of a soybean, do you?"

I shake my head, wondering where along the anger and fist-fight continuum Billy and Anna met.

"Oh, I have something for you," he says, patting my thigh and walking over to his desk where he picks up a postcard. "Meditation workshop this weekend. Specifically for healing. Okay if I slip it right in here?" He leans over my open bag, dangling the postcard. I nod and he drops it inside.

When he returns to my side he sets himself up behind my head, straddling his exercise ball. He sweeps my hair off the nape of my neck and rubs my cervical spine in gentle, sweeping motions. He says, "So homework—eat a burger, see how you feel and let me know next time. It'll give me something to look forward to." He places his hand over my forehead and I have a sudden vision of Billy and I kissing in a dark, tropical cove. I nearly let out a sigh, soaking up the insta-fantasy.

"That's it for today," he says, pressing his palm against my skull for a moment, then releasing me and sliding his hands together, maybe to hold onto my cellular residue. A girl can dream, right?

I slowly sit up and glance into his eyes, which betray a beaten down exhaustion I swear wasn't there before.

"Are you okay?" I ask. "You look—I don't know..."

"It's nothing," he says, which is clearly a lie. It probably has to do with Anna. Maybe he'll spill about the fight.

I slip on my boots, waiting.

"It's just Anna and me. We fought again."

"Oh, I'm sorry," I say, trying to look ignorant, and chastise myself for being secretly delighted that he chose to confide in me.

"She just got some new clients. She's kind of, I don't know. She's like, going crazy. I tell her she doesn't have to take on so much."

"Going crazy how?" I ask.

"She constantly wants to see them, she worries about them, she offers them free consultations. It's hard to rescue the world, you know?"

"Yeah," I say, jolted with a stab of envy for Anna, that she's so altruistic. That she's the type of person who, unlike me, would lay her own needs aside to help someone else. "She sounds like a really good person," I say, and try not to sigh.

"No. She is. You're right. I just wish she'd take it easy. She gets so intense."

As I gather my things and head for the door, I imagine all the frustrations and insults they may have hurled at each other last night.

I'm lost in thought when Billy adds, "Oh and, you might experience some loose stools for the next few days."

"Oh, sure!" I say, sprung from my reverie, and nearly trip over my feet on the way out.

Chapter 10

*I*n the minivan I inspect the postcard.

Befriend your inner monsters and transcend your limiting beliefs through guided meditation with Billy Dorian—Eastern Healer in the Western World. $50 suggested donation.

I brush my fingertips over the card. I've tried meditating but never got anywhere with it—no blue light visions, no earth-shattering revelations. Just a lot of itching and wishing I were somewhere else. Usually it's my eyebrows that get me. An irresistible urge overtakes me, to tweeze.

I press the card to my lips, then slip it into my bag and press play on the stereo.

I saw you there. Just standing there,
And I thought I was only dreaming yeah…

The car traverses the twists along Lincoln Drive.

I kiss you then. And once again,
You said you would come and dance with me

Dance with me, Across the sea,
We can feel the motion of a thousand dreams!

I still can't believe he is such a badass. With his motorcycle and his scars and his bastardy past.

Oh Doctor! Doctor! Can't you see I'm burning, burning?
Oh! Doctor! Doctor! Is this love I'm feeling?

A police car is parked at the curb when I get home. Glad to see they're watching out for the neighborhood, especially after one of our neighbors got robbed last month. Thieves made off with a wedding band, a string of fake pearls, two iPads, a MacBook Air and a bottle of Grey Goose—La Poire, if I remember correctly. I wonder if Anna knows about that. My cell rings. It's my mom. A sliver of irritation worms its way between my eyebrows as I cut the engine and press ANSWER.

"Hello my darling," she gushes into the phone. "Where were you when I called before? I was worried. I drove by your house."

"I'm fine, Mom," I sigh. A Japanese maple leaf releases its branch above the van and tendrils down to the windshield. "I was at the acupuncturist. I didn't hear it ring."

"Oh? Did he give you anything for the pain? You poor baby."

"He's not like that. He does bodywork. He's into meditation."

"Ooh, that sounds right up my alley. I keep meaning to go to that Shamalama place on Sansom Street but I keep getting caught up in other things."

"You mean the Shambhala center?"

"I guess," she says, as if remembering the correct name is beyond the scope of importance.

"What *things* do you keep getting caught up in?" I ask, digging my own shallow grave of aggravation.

"Oh you know. Book club, and laundry... Going to the periodontist."

"Mom, aren't you retired? You can go meditate in Tuscany if you want. You're free."

"I guess I could," she says, considering the possibility. "Eh, I'd rather go down the shore, to tell you the truth." She laughs.

"Seriously Mom, laundry? Periodontist? That's so depressing."

"Well thank you, dear. I'm glad my twilight years depress you. Maybe they'll inspire you to floss."

I groan. "I'm sorry."

"It's all right. But you really should floss. So what are you up to this weekend?"

"There's this workshop the, uh, healer guy said I should go to," I say, already giving her far too much information. That word *healer*. Gets stuck in my throat.

"What kind of workshop?"

"Meditation," I say slowly. I wince, anticipating the worst.

"That sounds very interesting. Where and when?" she pipes up, giddy.

"Hang on." I pull the postcard out of my bag, give my mother the information.

"Didn't you have a teacher named Dorian when you were little?" she asks.

"How do you remember that?" I say.

"Because he got arrested," she says. "Don't you remember? He killed his wife with a can of house paint. I think he taught art. The police found her chopped-up body in the Wynnewood shopping center. Bastard put her in a dumpster. In seven different garbage bags."

"Jesus Christ," I say. "How do I not know this?"

"Well, you were a kid when it happened. It was all over the news. Anyway, I'm sure it's not him. Unless your Dorian is an old man."

"He's in his thirties I think."

"Eh, maybe it's his son. Could you imagine? He was a handsome man. I remember that. Such a shame."

"Yeah, it would've been fine if he was ugly," I snark, but a shiver of fear courses through me at the phrase *handsome man.*

"That's not what I meant, Eve."

"I know."

"So, can I come with you?" she asks, hopeful as a puppy.

"Sure," I say, clamping my eyes shut.

"Is it a particular type of meditation? Because you know I used to study with what's-his-face back when you were a baby."

"Amrit Desai?"

"Amrit Desai," she repeats, pronouncing every syllable of Kripalu's founder completely differently than I just have. "Another charmer. What'd he do again? Sleep with his secretary?"

"I don't know. Sounds right. The yoga community is full of scoundrels," I say. "Anyway, this thing is all about healing and transcending. Billy said it would help with the pain."

"Ooh, I love healing and transcending. Will you pick me up and we can go together?"

I mouth the word FUCK at the windshield. "Of course I will," I say, wondering how I'll get any transcending done with my mother in the same room.

"Oh good, because then I don't have to figure out how to get there."

"No, I can do it for you."

"Oh, I can't wait. It will be so much fun, just the two of us. I've wanted to do something like this with you for the longest time," she says.

"Then why didn't you?" I ask.

"Oh you know," she says, trailing off.

"You were waiting for me to initiate," I say.

"Not at all," she says, offended.

"The laundry?" I say.

"The laundry," she says with a guffaw.

I utter my goodbyes into the phone and press END. I stare at the garage—our detached two-car garage. It sounded so ritzy in the realtor's description. It could be ritzy. Instead there's the peeling paint, the window Sam broke with a baseball bat, the streaks of gold spray paint the kids got a hold of one day when no one was watching. Weeds clamor for space in the crumbling driveway. I pull the key from the ignition, and trudge up the front steps.

Chapter 11

eil and a mustached officer with purple-veined cheeks and huge feet are talking in the living room when I enter. Weird. "What's going on?" I say, as Neil rushes into my arms, his face wrecked with tears. Really weird.

"Anna," he says, sobbing.

"What?" I say, having gone from leery to frantic in the space of two seconds. "What about Anna?"

"She's—"

"What? Neil, tell me!"

"Dead!" Neil blurts.

"Oh my God," I say. Then again. "Oh my God!" I begin to cry too and we clutch each other.

The officer flips a page in his narrow pad and scribbles something. "I'm sorry about all this Mrs. Myer. Would you like to have a seat? A glass of water?" I look at his badge. *G. Martucci*.

Neil goes to the kitchen and comes back with a glass of water for me.

"Does Billy know?" I ask.

"We've got an officer at his, uh, office," Martucci says. Then, "Mrs. Myer, do you mind if I ask you a couple questions?"

"Sure. But I mean, how did she—"

"She was found in the bathtub this morning by the nanny." As he says this, two more squad cars pull up outside. No sirens. She's already gone.

"Oh my God," I say again, looking out the window as the officers trudge across their front lawn. There is nothing else I can say. It's too surreal. Too terrible. "What about Deepak?"

Officer Martucci sips in a breath. Holds it.

"What about the baby?" I say, louder.

"He didn't make it, Mrs. Myer."

"What?" I say, standing up. "No! No! He's three! He can't not be alive!"

Neil breaks into a fresh set of sobs and we reach for each other again. Martucci scribbles again in his pad. "I'm sorry Mrs. Myer. Mr. Myer. Deepak—he and Ms. Lisko were found together."

"I can't—" I start. "I can't." I clutch at Neil and scream into his chest. An unmarked car pulls to the curb.

"Mrs. Myer, I know this is very difficult. But did you hear anything unusual from nine o'clock last night until this morning? Did you see anything? Not that we think there was foul play. It's just that, well, since the child was involved in the incident, we want to make sure, cover all bases. Just doing our jobs."

"Of course," I say, and watch as a female officer cordons off the Dorian house with plastic yellow tape that says, Police Line—Do Not Cross.

Neil is sitting on the sofa hugging himself and weeping softly when another officer appears at the door. I usher him inside. Officer Martucci introduces us to Officer Vale, a clean-shaven strawberry of a cop, all rounded and tufted and shoe-shined. "Okay if Officer Vale takes a look around?" Martucci asks.

"Sure," I say and watch as Vale starts inspecting our house, glancing out the window at the Dorian house, jotting in his notepad, lifting piles of bills and the kids' homework. I look at his gun, menacing and black and deadly, hitched to his hip. Part of his uniform. It unsettles me, the thought that he might use it someday, that he has hurt someone with it. "Is there some reason you're— not that I mind—we're happy to cooperate, but why are you—"

"As I said, Mrs. Myer. Just covering all our bases. So, did you see or hear anything unusual?"

I shake my head slowly, thinking back. "I put the kids to bed," I say. "I think I glanced out the window when Billy pulled into the driveway."

"You think or you did?"

"I did," I say in a small voice. I am always glancing out my window. Staring. Spying. Ogling.

"And when was that, Mrs. Myer?"

"Well, I put the kids to bed at eight-thirty, so it must have been around nine. I'd already had a cup of tea." And a bowl of ice cream.

"Go on, Mrs. Myer. This is very helpful. We appreciate your cooperation very much."

"I, uh. I saw them talking, through the window." I point lamely toward the kitchen where I do my spying.

"Any sign of an altercation?" the officer asks.

"No," I say quickly. But of course I'm lying. They were screaming at each other. "They were just talking," I say. "Maybe like, catching up after a long work day." A fresh wave of sobs washes over me then and I sink into the sofa next to Neil. "And he left again afterward."

"Billy left?"

"Yes. He drove away."

"Did he return?"

"Not that I saw," I say. "I went to bed." I got in bed and shoved my hand between my legs. "Does he know yet?" I ask.

"We've got a detective on the way to his office."

I nod, numb, imagining Billy's face when he finds out.

"Thank you for your cooperation, Mrs. Myer. I know this is very difficult. One last question for both of you. Any unusual vehicles pull up between nine o'clock last night and this morning?"

I shake my head. "Neil gets home around midnight," I say.

The officer looks at Neil. "Anything?" he asks my tormented husband.

Neil looks up at Officer Martucci and shakes his head.

Officer Martucci thanks Neil as he jots another note in his long pad. Then he flips it shut. "I think I have all I need for now. I'll be in touch if there's anything else." He looks at Vale, who approaches from the kitchen, holding a scrap of paper between his fingers.

"Did one of you write this?" Vale asks, holding out the paper, glancing at Officer Martucci. I take it from his hand wondering what—then I read it: *Part-time single mother gets shiny new neighbor. Homicidal bloodbath ensues.*

"I wrote it," I say, gulping, my brain suddenly swaddled in a layer of bubble wrap. "But it's fiction. It's just a—a story idea. I'm a writer. Well—trying to be. I—" My voice sounds like it's coming from the basement. The back yard. From a closed coffin.

Neil takes the receipt from my hand, reads over it. His eyes grow wide. "It says *bath*," he says and looks at me with alarm.

"Neil," I say. "You know I make this stuff up all the time."

"There's more?" Vale says. "Care to show us, Mrs. Myer?"

As I stand up I feel like my legs will give out from under me. I wipe my palms on my linty yoga pants. "I'll be right back," I say and sprint up the stairs.

First, in the bathroom, panting, I take in my reflection, wondering how far removed I look from a killer, how my face would look on a mug shot. Then I start collecting scraps of paper and cardstock littered with my scribblings. I grab everything I can with shaking hands and get to the top of the stairs when I remember. I run back to the bedroom and there on the wall is the Post-it about Anna's telepathic powers. I can't flush it. They'll hear. I can't let it sit in the trashcan. I stare at it and then tear it into confetti bits, shove them in my mouth and grab a swig of water from the tap in the bathroom. I run back downstairs swallowing, tears streaming down my face, and hand my pile to Vale.

He holds my pile of hostile musings and sorts through them, his eyebrows raising at a number of them. "Femurs for oars, huh?" he says, eyeing Martucci.

Martucci says, "Mrs. Myer, were you angry at Anna Lisko?"

"No!" I say, protesting. "She was very nice. I was just—a little—well you know. Women can get—envious. She was very, um, beautiful. And wealthy. And—I don't know. Self-possessed I guess. But I really liked her as I got to know her. I wanted to be friends. I would never do anything to hurt her."

"Did you think she was beautiful, Mr. Myer?" Officer Vale asks, turning to Neil.

Neil looks up from his weeping posture, afflicted. As if slapped. He looks at me. "I'm sorry, Eve," he says. Then he looks at the officers. "She was beautiful," he whispers. "But is that a crime?"

The officers look at each other and scribble in their notebooks. "Murder is a crime, Mr. Myer," says Martucci. "Thinking is not." He looks at Neil, as if waiting for him to crack and admit that he was in love with her, that he drowned her and Deepak because he was enraged that he couldn't have her all to himself. Then they look at me as if waiting for me to crack and confess that I was blind with jealous rage and determined to keep Anna and Neil apart no matter the cost.

I watch Vale sort once again through my story ideas, not sure if I feel more threatened by the prospect of being arrested for Anna and Deepak's murder, or by the possibility that he'll advise me not to quit my day job. Finally he says, "Okay with you if

I hold onto these, Mrs. Myer?" He flaps the papers in the air a couple times.

I nod and think, is it only guilty people who call lawyers? Am I making a mistake by handing them over? What would happen if I refused? What if I never get them back? I make a mental vow to start writing on the computer. Or buy a journal—an old school diary with a lock and key. Hide it under my mattress. In my underwear drawer, next to the vibrator.

When the officers finally leave, Neil turns to me and whispers, as if our house is bugged, "What were you thinking?"

"Are you kidding me?" I say. "It's a fucking story idea."

"*Homicidal bloodbath*, Eve? Why are you so angry at Anna?"

"You would be too," I mutter and stand from the sofa, wishing I could start a new collection, one where Neil would get it right between the eyes. "You better not suspect that I had anything to do with this. I swear to God, Neil. Our marriage will not survive one more shred of suspicion. You know I didn't do anything, right?" My stomach twists then and I clutch my middle, pleading silently for the paper scraps to stay down.

"Rick's truck pulled up after Billy left," Neil says, oblivious to my churning guts as I curl into a ball on the sofa. "Around one."

"What? Why didn't you say anything?" I ask him, panicking again. "They might come back for me!"

"They're such a nice family," he says, and opens his palms to the ceiling, a single tear rolling down his blotched face.

"What about me, Neil? Am I nice family?" I say, propping myself on an elbow.

"Sam, Chloe," I say, looking at my angels through puffy eyes at dinner that night. "Mommy and Daddy have something important to tell you." This was the plan from the beginning, to tell the kids the truth about life. Not to candy-coat it. We don't want them growing up only to feel gypped. Better to be prepared as soon as possible—disappoint them in their formative years so they can handle the grand anticlimax of existence when they grow up.

"This morning, Anna and Deepak—" Neil says, and sobs. "I can't." He's taken the day off from work.

"Kids, they died," I blurt. Looking at them, the world flips, becoming instantly surreal. I feel like I am playing a practical joke.

The kids' eyes are huge. Sam looks frightened. Chloe looks at her big brother to gauge how she is supposed to react. To see if Mommy is serious. Sam bursts into tears. Chloe looks afraid. But then she smiles. "No they didn't," she says. "They didn't died."

"They did, sweetie. I'm so sorry. Do you want a hug?"

"Mommy, what if a stick could talk to you?" she says, and I shake my head at my daughter. Her undeveloped brain has saved her from yet another despair. Lucky girl.

"Why did they die?" Sam says, and Neil pulls him onto his lap, squeezes him and cries into his little shoulder.

"It was an accident," I say. Which is hopefully true. Just a mom who fell asleep in the bathtub, and a little boy who loved his mommy but couldn't swim. That's how I picture it. Neat, tidy. Purely accidental. It's the simplest explanation.

Later, Neil says, "Thank you. You were really good back there. I couldn't do it."

"It's fine," I say. "I guess today was their day."

"Their day for what?"

"To learn that people die, even little kids, and that life isn't fair."

"If anything like that ever happened to—" he starts, but doesn't finish.

"I've been thinking that all day."

"How can he go on? How can he take a single step? I can't imagine."

"I know. It's too much. Do you think it's too soon to bring him food?"

At first I Google. For once it turns out my mother was right—Billy Dorian's father bludgeoned his wife to death with a paint can. In 1976. My eyes sweep over the handful of articles that describe the "Bryn Mawr Bludgeoning." I sit there for days. Hours. Some inordinate stretch of time. I sit there until my eyes sting, until I need to take a shower and try to forget everything I've just seen.

I bake to keep myself away from the computer. It's the only thing that makes what happened bearable. As I measure, pour, stir and spoon, I replay the shouting match I witnessed. Billy walked into the house already fuming, and Anna did not seem surprised. They fought as if it was their usual way of interacting. At one point Deepak came running into the kitchen sobbing, followed by Julie, who swept him into her arms. The boy kicked and arched his back against his nanny as she scuttled out of the room, looking haggard and disheveled.

I make macaroons and merengues. Tollhouse cookies, a flourless chocolate cake, and gingersnaps. I make a plate for Neil and the kids and bring the rest over to Billy. I don't have the guts to ring the bell. Not yet. But I leave foil-wrapped plates on his porch. It gives me a sliver of an illusion that I have any control over anything. It feels so wrong for Anna and Deepak to be dead that it hurts physically. It doesn't matter that she was a beautiful, ridiculous, high-maintenance life-coach with telepathic powers. What matters is that she was human, with a heart and desires and fears. And a child. The most beautiful little boy. It breaks my heart into a million pieces knowing that he'll never grow up. That no one will get to watch as he learns to ride a bike and tell a stupid joke or grow obsessed with Harry Potter or soccer or swimsuit models. It's so fucking unfair. I can't stop wishing it weren't true. I can't stop asking why. I can't stop wanting this all to be a horrible dream. And I go to sleep weighed down with the knowledge. And when I wake up I feel light. For literally a second. And then the memory bashes me over the head and the heaviness seeps in like flood water and sinks me to the bottom.

I call the police to see if there's any more information, to glean whether or not I will be arrested—if I should pack my tooth-brush—but they can't tell me anything other than, *Sit tight, Mrs. Myer. We're doing the best we can.* No one raps on the door in the middle of the night to take me away. I sleep fitfully, and pray every night that it will all be over soon—a Nor'easter that barely touched us after all.

Then I see Billy. I watch from my darkened bedroom as he returns home from his office. I place a chair in front of my window and watch him walk up the front stairs of his house, hanging his head, picking up the plates I've left. I sit with my knees tucked to my chin, my arms wrapped around them, and I watch him enter and I watch him sink to the floor and sob, and I feel like I am intruding, trespassing, but watching him fall apart soothes me somehow because his loss is bigger and more potent and some-how that shames me and comforts me at the same time. I huddle, wrapped in an old cashmere sweater. I watch him and wish there was something I could do. I wish I could bring back his son and even his wife. I wish I could know what he and Anna were fighting about that night.

Rick and Beth arrive at Billy's and I watch the brothers cry while Beth stands away from them, as if their tears are a virus she might catch if she gets too close. I study Rick for signs of homicidal tendencies, and Beth for signs of the same—or relief—but I can't trust my eyes or my brain. Every wire feels crossed. Every synapse dulled and frayed.

No one bothers with the curtains. Chinese food containers pile up on the kitchen counter. Casserole dishes. Makes me wonder where Julie is, but only for a second, because what does a single guy with no kids need a nanny for? She didn't have a car. She used Anna's Mercedes. But the car just sits in the driveway unused.

I finally ring the bell, cradling a Mason jar filled with home-made granola, a container of pistachio fudge and a six-pack of Sam Adams. Billy and I stand there in the doorway staring at each other. He takes the food and beer from my arms, sets it down on a narrow table in his entryway. "I'm so sorry," I say, and start to cry again.

"I know," he says, and he cries too.

I hold out my arms because it's the only thing I feel that's true and I don't care if he walks away or walks into my arms. But he does walk into my arms, and we stand there embracing and sob-bing and I keep saying, "I'm so sorry. I'm so sorry," and I stroke the back of his hair and there's a moment when I feel like his lover and the next moment we let go of each other and glance into each other's eyes and then avert our gazes. We're completely wet and red and ruined and he asks me to come in and he eats a couple squares of fudge and even compliments them. We have a beer together.

"It's just unbelievable," he says. He says it a few times, staring into space.

"I know. It's surreal," I say. "When you know someone. And love them. And they're not there anymore. Just this—absence. I can't imagine how hard it must be for you. When I heard—I just couldn't. I couldn't believe it."

"Yeah, it's surreal all right. She was a good soul. She made the world a better place."

I study his profile, looking for clues—of what, I'm not sure. Who says after their wife dies that she was a good soul? It seems detached somehow. *She made the world a better place.* I think back to when Neil and I fell in love, when I was a senior in college. If he'd died in the throes of our honeymoon period, when we used to fuck five times a day and couldn't stop grinning at each other between orgasms, I wouldn't have said in a million years that he was a good soul. I would have curled up in the fetal position for a year, keening and moaning.

"God, I sound like a Hallmark card," he says, as if reading my thoughts.

"She was good though," I say. "I barely knew her, but I could see how much she cared. She was great about my whole back thing, and she adored Deepak. I am—so sad about—" I start to cry again.

"It makes no sense that she would do this," he says.

"You think it was—" I can't say the word.

"Suicide? I don't know. I keep thinking, she was distraught over her job. We were fighting—a lot. She was definitely not herself the last few days. And Deepak—" Billy sobs. "He had his pajamas on. Like he crawled in to save her—" He can barely get the words out. "And I wasn't there!"

"It's not your fault," I say.

"It's not fair," Billy says, wiping his nose, which is now red and swollen. "I've spent half my life dealing with how useless that concept is. What's fair and what's not fair. There's no such thing, really, you know? Life is something that just comes at you. You either ride it or you're screwed. As soon as you start believing in fair and unfair, that leads to justice, injustice, intolerance, resentment, revenge. I've watched that—fallacy—destroy people I love. You become a prisoner of your own limited thinking. A belief system that someone else handed down to you blindly. And yet all I can think of is how fucking unfair it is that Deepak is gone and I wasn't there."

"He was young. And vibrant. And funny," I say. "How could

you not feel that way? It's got to be hard-wired into your brain or something. He was—I mean I barely knew him, and I can't stand kids—"

This makes us laugh through our tears.

"But I just fell in love with him, you know?"

"He's got that thing," Billy says.

After that the only thing I can think of to say is, "He was just the cutest little man." I pause, take a steadying breath and add— "He looked just like you." I say it because I want him to know I think highly of him, that I respect his pain, but as soon as the words are out of my mouth I know I shouldn't have said them.

And when Billy says, "What do you mean?" in this hostile tone I've never heard before, I'm sure I've said too much. There's a storm in his eyes, darkening them. His brows draw together and his jaw tenses. He rubs his face and I wish I could hug him but I feel light years away.

I say, panicking, "I mean that he looked like you. What did you think I meant?"

And the cloud passes and he looks at me with kindness restored. He says, "Forget it."

And I'm suddenly kicking myself because he obviously thinks I just hit on him in his time of mourning and I am the biggest fool in the universe and all I wanted to do was be there for him. "I'm sorry," I say. "I didn't mean to say anything—to make you—to—" but I don't know what the rest of that sentence would entail. I'm just plain old sorry.

"It's okay, Eve," Billy says, and smoothes a hand over my leg and the skin beneath my jeans electrifies despite my efforts against this attraction. "I've been such a mess. I didn't mean to snap at you. You're a—you've been a really good—" he looks into my eyes and the tears start rolling all over again. "I just miss him so much," he sobs, and rests his head in my lap, which along with the fact that he did not say 'I just miss *them* so much' floods my veins with adrenaline.

I stroke his hair, allowing my tears to fall in his ringlets, on his cheekbone, on his nose. I swipe them away with a finger. I cry because I am so sad for this suddenly alone man, and I cry because in a fraction of a lifetime, I've grown inexplicably fond of him, in a way that scares the shit out of me.

Chapter 12

~c˙ɔ~

W hy didn't you tell the police about Rick's car?" I ask Neil in the front yard when I return home from yoga, going about my usual routine despite the news. I don't know what else to do, now that I've exceeded my quota for crying and staring into space.

Neil's raking leaves, wearing gardening gloves and old jeans. The set of his brow tells me he remains steeped in misery like a forgotten tea bag.

"Because—well, at first it was because I wanted to stay out of it. Then I realized I could be hindering the investigation. I'm going to call the police and let them know."

"Are you going to be, I don't know, arrested for lying to the police?"

"I don't know, Eve. But it's the right thing to do."

"When are you going to call them?"

"I'll call them from work."

"Did Billy say anything else to you that night?" I ask.

He shakes his head. "Eve, I was so beat. I really don't remember anything else."

"Think, Neil. Did he say anything about Deepak, or Anna, or Rick?"

"Just that he'd had a hard day. That was all." His raking picks up speed.

"And what about Rick driving up? Besides not saying anything about it, what do you think?"

"Eve, Jesus. I didn't make too much of it since he was such a blowhard at the party. I thought, I don't know. He's obviously obsessed with that house. And then I thought about what you think you saw, and thought I'd stay out of it."

"What *I think* I saw?"

"What you saw. Jesus, Eve."

"So then why didn't you say anything? I don't understand."

"Eve, just drop it. I fucked up, okay?" Neil throws his rake down.

"Okay." I take a step back. Exhale. As hard as Neil is working, the yard is still covered with leaves. The big old scarlet oak refuses to relent. It looms over our yard, daring Neil to complete his Sisyphean task.

"Well, do you think we could grill Saturday?" I say, shifting from foot to foot.

"I'll go to the store and buy some garden burgers." He walks toward the garage, emerges a few moments later with a jumbo lawn bag from the township.

"Actually, I think we should grill beef burgers," I say when he resumes his raking.

He looks at me then. "I thought we were trying to be vegetarians." He scratches his ear, leaving a sooty smudge.

"The, uh, Billy told me. He told me to eat meat. You know, if I crave it."

"Did you know Billy's dad bludgeoned his wife to death?" he says.

"Did my mom tell you that?"

"It's all over the news, Eve. Billy's mother was murdered by his father. Do you not think that fucks a person up for life?"

"Oh, so now he's evil," I say, but have to admit that I hadn't even considered it until now, how completely fucked up his childhood must have been.

Neil's rake tears at the ground. Leaves swirl around us. Then he drops the rake again, rests his hands on his hips and looks at me. I mean, he *really* looks at me. It does not feel like the gaze of a man who loves you and wants to share his life with you. It feels more like the gaze of a man who wants to boil you alive. I'm about to walk away when he speaks. "You're so susceptible to other peoples' agendas. You take them on as your own without researching, as if you were a blank slate just waiting to be filled. You're impulsive."

"I researched this!" I explode. "I Googled!"

"Impulsive," he says, pointing at my convenient demonstration. He shakes his head. "You can't just fall for every new philosophy, Eve. We can't afford your whims."

"You have the audacity to talk to me about whims? About being impulsive?"

"Why don't you just divorce me, Eve? Get it over with."

"Because we can't afford it," I spit.

Neil flinches. Drops his rake. Then grabs it from the ground. His nose is red.

"So we'll eat vegetable burgers," I sigh. "Fine."

"His wife is dead. His mother is dead. His *child* is dead. You need to stay away from him. That's all I'm saying," he says.

"He wasn't even there!" I say.

"Maybe he came back," he hisses.

"Well, you lied to the police!"

"Which crime is worse, Eve?" he asks, his tone vicious.

"Billy Dorian did not kill his wife and kid," I say, filling with righteous justice. "I've had two sessions with him. Three hours. He's the nicest, most decent guy. And honest. And he *was not there.*"

"Will you just promise me that you'll stay away from him?"

"I don't know," I say, not wanting to give up this new friendship or yield to my husband's demands like an oppressed wife in a war-torn desert.

Neil says, "If he were ugly would you stay away? Are you that attracted to him?"

I open my mouth to tell Neil to shut the fuck up but no sound comes out, so I turn and walk away. As I stomp to the Minivan I hear a faint *go fuck yourself* rolling on the wind. It hits me like a brick through a window. Then I hear his rake tearing at the ground.

My yoga pants are damp with sweat. *I am not a blank slate.* I start the engine and tear out of the driveway, scattering leaves in my wake. *Asshole.* Before I know it, I'm parked on Jeannie's cramped little street, wondering if Billy could possibly—no. It's not. He could not. I walk up the concrete steps and ring her bell, hoping she's home, and I start sobbing the second she opens the door. "I'm sorry," I say through my tears. "I know this is horrible. You're busy. I should have called."

"Oh my God," she says, dressed in a chenille bathrobe, wet hair slicked back and dripping onto her shoulders. We embrace and I start crying harder. Jeannie says, "I was just considering having a shot of bourbon."

"I wrote horrible things about her," I blubber.

"What? What things, Eve? About who?"

I tell my sister about my writing, and the police.

"Well, did they take you in for questioning?"

I shake my head.

"Then you're probably clear. Don't worry, Eve."

I nod. Jeannie hands me a tissue and I blow my nose. Then something tumbles to the floor upstairs.

"Griffin's home from school today," she says, irritation darkening her cheeks.

"Is he sick?"

"Threw up all over me this morning. I was trying to get his ass in the car when it happened."

"Mom!" cries a raspy voice from upstairs.

I rumple my face in sympathy. "Poor kid," I say.

"I love him so much more when he's at school," Jeannie says. "I'll be right up!" she bellows at the staircase. Then she says to me, "You know where the bourbon is? I'll only be a minute."

"Sure. Tell him I hope he feels better," I say as she jogs up the stairs, her heavy footfalls vibrating the whole house.

Jeannie's place is a mess, worse than mine. Magazines piled everywhere, toys littering the floor, a mountain of DVDs and video games on the TV console. After I get the bourbon from the cabinet above her stove, I grab a couple glasses and clear a space on the dining room table. It reminds me of the bottom of a canyon, with books piled high on either side—*A Thousand Names for Joy*, *Walden*, *The Alchemist*, and dozens more.

"That boy, I swear," Jeannie says when she returns, now dressed in plum colored yoga pants and a baggy sweater that looks like it's covered in dog hair even though she has no pets. Then she changes the subject, picks up her glass. "What the fuck," she says, and shakes her head.

"I still can't believe it," I say. "I keep trying to picture how I'd feel if only Anna—I think I'd feel a little less—horrible, you know? Is that terrible to say?"

Jeannie takes my hand and rubs it. "I know," she says. "It's just, when it's a kid like that, it's just—"

"Is it really all over the news about Billy's dad?" I say, and Jeannie slides her laptop out from under a stack of magazines. I come around to her side of the table. She Googles "Dorian," "murder" and "1976." There are dozens of articles that mention the 1976 incident, the so-called "Bryn Mawr Bludgeoning." We browse a few and then see one entry for Richard Dorian Sr. on Wikipedia. Jeannie clicks on it. Under the heading "Murder," it says,

On August 23, 1976, Richard Dorian Sr. attacked his wife, Justicia Dorian (née Kanneman), youngest daughter of Philadelphia department store chain owner Joe Kanneman, with an unopened one-gallon paint can, resulting in her death. The Dorians had one child together, William, in 1973. At the time of the murder the three-year-old was asleep inside the house, as was the family's nanny, Ms. Julie Parraga. Fifteen-year-old Richard Jr., Dorian's son with first wife Marci Berman, was spending the night at a friend's house. During court testimony, Ms. Parraga stated that she and William slept through the night and heard no commotion. Justicia's dismembered body was found one week after the murder in a dumpster behind Kanneman's Wynnewood store.

Dorian, an art teacher at Penn Wynne Elementary School, was charged with murder by the Montgomery County, Pennsylvania District Attorney. Richard Sr. expressed remorse during his trial, drawing repeated portraits of his deceased wife, but pleaded not guilty to the charges. Lower Merion police indicated that Justicia had made more than 30 calls to the police in the three years she and Richard Sr. were married, from their house in Bryn Mawr. Neighbors claimed that on numerous evenings, shouting could be heard coming from the Dorian residence. Justicia had signed a complaint against Dorian after one hospital stay, but later dropped the complaint.

The case became a cause célèbre for the feminist movement due to the allegations of long-term domestic violence and the grisly nature of the attack — Justicia's head suffered from repeated blows and most bones in her body were shattered, indicating that the beating continued well after the victim was already dead. Gloria Steinem and *Ms. Magazine* helped raise money for Philadelphia-area women's shelters. *Ms. Magazine* reported that when Justicia called the police, officers would often discuss hunting with Dorian, as he was an avid sportsman with a large collection of animal trophies on display in various rooms in his residence. The amassed collection was an alleged cause of continuous friction between the couple, one neighbor reporting that Richard Sr. threatened to "put Justicia's head above the mantel if she didn't watch her step." It was later revealed that Justicia had been involved in an extramarital affair with a fellow faculty member at Bala Cynwyd Middle School, where she taught eighth grade history.

A panel of psychiatrists in a sanity hearing found Sr. Richard Dorian to be of sound mind and body, but determined that he suffered from compounded depression and post-traumatic stress stemming from an abusive past that included repeated molestation. Dorian later confessed to the murder and cooperated at every level of the proceedings, but insisted that he hit Justicia no more than three times. This testimony was later dismissed and he confessed to striking her after he was certain she was dead. He was found to be guilty of murder in the second degree and served twenty years—a minimum sentence due to his otherwise upstanding reputation in the community—at the Montgomery County Correctional Facility.

In addition to his abstract paintings, Richard Dorian completed a book of drawings while serving his prison term, dedicated to his late wife. It was published by Rizzoli in 2009 and garnered critical acclaim. Dorian committed suicide in January 2010 in his apartment in Ardmore, Pennsylvania.

"Jesus," I say.

"Fucking wack-job," Jeannie says.

Richard Sr., even with a seventies-style mustache and a wide-lapelled corduroy blazer, is a spitting image of Rick, with the long face to compensate for all those huge teeth, the wiry yellow hair, and the arrogant gleam in his eye. I think back to the little house tour Rick gave, how Neil leaned over at one point and whispered in my ear, "Do you think he'll let us go before the sun comes up?"

"Everyone's saying Billy killed her because she was having an affair," Jeannie says.

"Do they say who Anna was having an affair with?" I say, refilling our glasses.

Jeannie Googles "Anna Lisko affair." There is no mention of Rick as far as any affair. *An unnamed man*, the articles say. I think of Rick's gold watch. His shiny truck. The money he must have to pay people off to not mention his name in cyberspace.

We do learn that Justicia Dorian was planning to leave Richard Sr. for a man named John Vallone, the Bala Cynwyd school guidance counselor. They'd been secretly meeting for over a year.

"I still don't get it," I say. "Why the baby?"

"That's what they said on the morning show. You should really get a TV."

"That's the last thing I need. I'd never get anything done. You know how I am." Then I tell Jeannie about seeing Rick and Anna in the driveway.

"So Anna's just like Billy's dead mother," Jeannie says. "Fucking homewreckers."

"Yeah but why would anyone cheat on Billy? He's so—"

"Yes?"

"Jeannie, he is the most exquisite man I have ever laid eyes on."

"Exquisite, huh. Well, maybe his brother Rick has a bigger cock."

I don't tell her about the fight I witnessed. The thought of incriminating Billy. I can't do it. And I don't mention Rick's car either. Neil lied to the police. *But then again, so did I.* "And Billy's so nice," I say. "He's wrecked over the whole thing. How could he do a thing like that?"

"Because it's always the husband, Eve," Jeannie says, sipping her drink.

"Meanwhile, I don't understand why it has to be anyone. She drowned in the bathtub. Billy himself said that she's been depressed. Distraught. That is not murder. Maybe Deepak really did get in there to try and wake her up or something. And just, I don't know, slipped.

"You know, there was a woman where I used to work—at that library in Brooklyn. Her sister drowned in the bathtub. Fell asleep. No drugs. Nothing. And there was no murder investigation. People thought it was suicide but eventually it was ruled an accident. So why can't this be the same? Occam's razor and all that shit."

"Because of Deepak," Jeannie says. "And people, especially around here, are bored. They love gossip and drama. This story is too good not to go crazy with, especially with the paint can thing. And if you weren't tight with Billy, if you didn't know him well enough to feel sorry for him, if he weren't so *exquisite*, you'd be all over it too." My sister smiles at me and takes a victorious swallow of her bourbon.

"Well, there is one other thing," I say.

My sister raises her eyebrows.

"What would you think if I told you that Anna was telepathic?"

Chapter 13

~c̃ɔ~

A nna's car smells like a million dollar bill. Billy is using it today, taking it out of retirement before he sells it to the highest bidder. He's offered to drive me, Jeannie and my mother to the meditation workshop, which is on after being postponed for a month. Billy says it's the only way he can function, by doing his job. It will be special though—a memorial meditation. From the looks of him though, functioning is not the word that comes to mind, since he's dressed even more casually than usual, in loose drawstring pants and a T-shirt with a faded yin-yang symbol on the front. His face is unshaven and his hoodie has stains on it—toothpaste from the looks of it. When I glance at his feet I see that he's wearing bedroom slippers, and he's got some schmatta in his hair, like a headband. And yet, he's the only guy in a five-mile radius who could pull off a head scarf and bunny slippers and still look insanely hot.

With my mom in the front seat regaling Billy with her riveting medical wocs, I phone Jeannie to let her know of the change of plans, but she's on call so she's out. "Shit," I say, then whisper: "You're going to leave me alone at a healing workshop with mom?"

"You won't be alone, Eve. You'll have the *exquisite* suspected wife and baby killer. It's all good. Oh and by the way, I was thinking about the telepathy thing and at first I was like, well, that's it. Someone wanted to stop Anna from seeing something. But then I was like—" She stops short.

"What? Tell me." I sneak a glance at Billy to see if he can somehow hear Jeannie on the other end, but he's busy receiving an earful about my mother's suspicious mole.

"It's just impossible, Eve," Jeannie says. "Her charisma, beauty—something must have just knocked your brains loose. I've seen you like this before. Remember when you were sure you could levitate?"

"You mean 'Light as a feather, stiff as a board?' Jeannie, I was seven years old!"

"Seven? Really? I thought you were a lot older. Anyway, it has to have been a suicide. You know, with a very unfortunate accident. Because she's not the type who would hear God's voice telling her to kill her kid, right? But I gotta go. More haggling with the OT over the CS. Let's talk tomorrow."

I hang up, fully dejected that my own sister thinks I'm a schmuck to believe that Anna had special powers. At least she doesn't think she was psychotic.

"This car is wonderful," my mother is saying to Billy, fondling the burled walnut console. "You can't fake high quality."

"Thank you Mrs. Shankin. It is a good car," Billy says. Meanwhile my mother drives her 2000 Honda Civic to Wal-Mart for generic cranberry juice.

"I am so sorry about your loss," she says. "How are you even functioning?"

"Not very well," he admits, gripping the steering wheel.

My mother begins quizzing Billy on his credentials. When he tells her he studied in China, she says, "Well then we know we can trust you. That is the real deal." Billy shoots her a glance and I slap my mom on the shoulder from the back seat where I'm huddled.

My mom swats away her gaffe, and pats Billy's thigh. "I didn't mean it like that," she says, but it doesn't end there. Her social anxiety wouldn't be complete if she didn't sell me down the river. "I would have loved for Eve to travel more, but she was set on pursuing acting." My mother flails her hands and head around, as if to illustrate how flighty and impractical I am.

Billy nods and turns to my mother. "Mrs. Shankin, would you mind if we didn't talk for the rest of the ride?"

From where I sit I can see the pink rose of shame bloom on my mother's left cheek. She has been chastened by a suspected— by meddling neighborhood gossips anyway—murderer. She keeps her mouth clamped shut for the rest of the ride, her chin wobbling slightly but held defiantly high.

I settle back into my seat and stare at the back of Billy's head. Neil was relieved at the very least that I'm not going alone with Billy. "I can't force you to do the right thing," he'd said as I got my things together. We didn't kiss goodbye. We barely touch anymore.

But since the autopsy results have yet to be submitted to the police, the community is going crazy playing whodunit guessing games that I overhear at the kids' school, where at least no one suspects me to my face. They all think Billy did it. "There's something in his eyes," one of them said, as if she could see into his soul, as if her pronouncement would hold up in court.

And at Trader Joe's I heard my name mentioned more than once by yentas who don't—well, who don't know me from Eve. "I heard Eve Myer was hitting on Billy at the housewarming," one of them said. "You know my book group friend Sara? Her cousin is friends with Rick's wife. Apparently Eve nearly got Deepak run over by a car that night." Her cart was filled with fat-free Greek yogurt, skim milk, baby spinach and rice cakes.

A second one agreed. "How nauseating," she said, opening a

box of dark chocolate-covered edamame and popping a couple into her lipsticked lie hole. "She sounds like a freak."

I wondered why they never thought I might be in line behind them, listening to their every word. "I heard Eve saved Deepak's life that night," I said, butting in, white-knuckling the handles of my shopping basket, figuring that despite my nerves I had nothing to lose. "And that Billy was flirting with Eve." I add this, because why not? It's fucking true.

"That is not true," the diet yenta said. "I heard it from someone who was *there* that night."

The chocolate soybean said, "As if it's any of your business," fingering her next mouthful.

"You're probably right," I said, holding out my hand. "Eve Myer. Nice to meet you. Oh and by the way, I *love* your boots. Did you get them at PayLess?" There's nothing that offends a rich bitch more than mistaking her expensive crap for cheap crap.

The yentas gaped at me in horror, shaking in their scrunched and buckled monstrosities.

"You might want to watch what you say about me," I went on, heady with power, adrenaline coursing through my every cell. "You never know what could happen to you when you're home alone."

"Are you threatening us?" the chocolate soybean said.

"No more than you're threatening me. You want to drag my name through this shitstorm, then you better be prepared to pay the price. You have no idea what's going on. You believe every little shred of gossip you hear. You're pathetic."

"You're insane," the diet yenta said, indignant.

"You're a cunt," I whispered, putting my face right up to her overly made up mug. "And you look like a cheap whore."

By the time I finished paying for my broccoli and grass-fed beef, my hands were shaking so badly I could barely slide my card through the little machine thing. But I felt more alive than I had in years.

♉

When we arrive at the studio, a small crowd is gathered outside. At first I think it's attendees waiting to come in but then I see the signs, the cop cars and a couple police barricades. We're instructed by a few officers to form a line against the brick storefronts, except for Billy, who's escorted inside among the loudest shouting.

The protestors have been cordoned behind the barricades, off the curb. They take up two parking spaces but make a hell of a racket. They're mostly moms like me. I recognize Roxann Gottlieb and her PTA cronies—busybodies in pastel fleece jackets, tacky sunglasses and bad dye jobs who have nothing better to do than stir up trouble. These are the moms who hassle teachers and school principals, demand lower speed limits, complain about overgrown hedges, unraked leaves and boys with sticks, like my Sam. Threats lurk everywhere to these hovercrafty bores, and now, with a baby dead and suspects to blame, they're out for blood.

"Honor the innocent!" They chant, poking signs in the air that read, *Baby-killer!* And—*Save our CHILDREN!*

Roxann catches my eye and mouths the words, "You're disgusting."

Nausea blooms in my gut. I've ignored Roxann for the past two years, to no avail, avoiding her loud-mouth rants about everything from the treacherous, unacceptable carpool line to the horribly unqualified gifted program teacher, to the exasperating unavailability of Asics sneakers on Zappos for her darling Hadley whose feet are so narrow!

Blood rises in my chest and before I know it, I'm storming over to her.

"My life is none of your goddamned business," I say, when I reach her at the police barricade.

Roxann's lower jaw unhinges, leaving her lips tracing a tight circle. One of the PTA droogs comes to the rescue, her stork legs clad in a sad pair of fake True Religion jeans and square-toed brown leather boots. "We're just protecting our own," she says, flashing her garish pink French manicure and an undermining scowl. The self-righteousness emanates from her like a virus. Her shiny blow-dried bob shimmers with the stuff.

"Get a fucking life," I tell Roxann, glare at the PTA goon, and rejoin the line of people waiting to enter the studio. I should have thrown her to the ground and stomped on her ugly-ass head. But I am too enlightened for that.

Once our line starts to move, two moist-eyed attendants at the door wearing T-shirts printed with a photo of Anna and Deepak hand out daisies—Anna's favorite, I learn. Inside the studio, we walk down a makeshift center aisle and place the flowers at the foot of a poster of Anna, a professional-looking shot of her practicing dancing shiva pose on a rock somewhere in pristine nature. She smiles into the middle distance, holding her foot high up behind her back with both hands, her upper body a narrow, perfect U shape demonstrating an unnecessary amount of flexibility, her lightly freckled face tan and serene. Anna is beautiful, happy—a bright soul. I can see that in the picture. I feel terrible for ever resenting her. I still can't believe she's gone. That Deepak is gone. The disbelief crops up a few times a day, even as life begins to resume its former texture. I place my daisy in a growing mountain of frothy yellow and white, and find a spot for my mother and me in the crowded studio.

I help her with a mat and pillow I've brought from home while she goes on and on about the ruckus outside. "Don't they have anything better to do?" she says, lowering herself to the floor. "They should come in here and get their minds straight. Picking on that poor, poor man."

"Thanks, Mom," I say, impressed with her clarity.

"Well, at least wait until the autopsy results are in before accusing the man of murder." A few people turn to glare. I should have known my mother's logic was too good to last.

I hush her and whisper, "Do you really think he did it?"

"Eve, I have no idea," she says. "For all we know she did it her-self. Suicide-murder. You know how women are these days with all their post-partum crap."

"You had a lot of your own crap, if I recall," I remind her, but I have to admit that once in a while the woman makes sense. I hold onto this barely plausible nugget of post-partum possibility as my mom surveys the room. Some of the older participants have cushiony seats with attached backrests. My mother points at one and says, "Oh, I wish I had one of those." Then she turns to me and asks, "Do I look all right?"

"You look fine," I say. "What are you going to do, go home and change?" I try not to look too closely at her ancient tubesocks, the jeans with the hole in the knee, the sweater that looks as if she scraped it from the side of the road. The thing with my mother is that she hates shopping or being in a situation that calls for socially acceptable behavior, so she's been dressing for the walls of her apartment ever since I went off to college, and she's still wearing the same rags twenty years later. I see it as social anxiety. She sees it as everyone else's problem until she finds herself in a well-lit room full of decently dressed people.

"I would if I drove," she says. "There might be cameramen here. We could be on the news." There is a hint of anticipation in her tone. "I wish I'd washed my hair," she says, stroking it with shaky fingers. "I think I'm the oldest one in the place."

"I think that guy is older," I whisper, pointing at an elderly man across the room. I regard my mother's oily auburn-dyed hair and the swipe of Vaseline on her cheekbones. It's her moisturizer of choice, and though she looks years younger than seventy-nine, I am reluctant to venture too close lest I get slimed. I have spied lint and hair in her gleam.

"Yeah, but he's bald," she says. "It doesn't count." She cracks up at her joke.

A woman in front of us turns and shushes us. My mother huffs her cheeks and sneaks her the finger when she turns back around and I hiss at her to behave, jarred by the sensation that I am talking to one of my children.

I'm having trouble keeping my eyes closed because my mother's prattle has seeped into my bones and it's making me jumpy. "I wish I'd worn sweatpants," she says. And, "Your sister works too hard. She should be here with us." And, "Oh Eve, this is such a horrible, horrible occasion but it is so *nice* to be here with you!" When her cell phone bursts into a samba I feel my face turn livid. Instead of turning it off she answers it—loudly. Amidst angry stares from all around she tells the caller, her lifelong friend whose name curiously enough is Yoyo, that she can't talk because she's "at a very interesting meditation memorial for that poor woman and her baby who drowned. Ugh so sad. We're meditating. We're memorializing. Yo, you should really be here. You love yoga."

"A good reminder to us all to switch our cell phones off," says Billy from the front of the room when my mother finally hangs up.

"I'm so sorry about that," my mom says to him, fumbling for her phone's switch. "I completely forgot to turn it off."

Billy puts a finger to his lips.

My mother opens her mouth to respond, her jaw hanging, quavering.

"No more talking," he says.

She looks like a scolded child. I place an arm on hers to stop her from making one more sound. She clutches her heart with a veiny hand. "I'm sorry!" she wails. "It's just so sad! The baby! Why the baby?"

Everyone's eyes are on her. Billy makes his way through the crowd and crouches down beside her, hitching up the thighs of his pants. My mother tucks her chin to her chest and whimpers, "Please don't hurt me."

Chapter 14

〜⟨⟩〜

Billy asks those of us surrounding my mother to make space, asks my mother to stand while he rearranges her things, spreading out her yoga mat. She appears as if naked, the only person in the room on her feet while everyone gawks. She strokes her hair over and over and smiles awkwardly. "I'm so sorry," she says, addressing the room. "I really didn't mean to interrupt—" Billy turns to her, a finger to his lips once again. Then he invites her to lie down on her back. "I feel so bad," she says, creaking to the floor. "I'm so embarrassed. I should get a new phone that's easier to turn off—" He shushes her again and she obeys like a submissive puppy.

"We're not here to explain," he says. "Explanations are a filter. They keep us from clarity. From the truth. Explanations, excuses and analyses keep us imprisoned in a cell made of lies that cause us great pain, that lead to decisions we come to regret. We're going to try to experience life as it is. Simply. Quietly. No filters in this room. Everybody got that?" Nods all around. When she's finally prone he places a hand over her heart. "Heart chakra," he says to the rest of us. "It doesn't matter what you call it, but for our purposes we'll call it that. Anyway it's where the pain lives." He presses on my mother's heart chakra and a wracking sob escapes her lips that causes a ripple of gasps around the room. "It's home to healing too," he adds. "Very powerful, right?" he asks us and every head in the room bobs up and down, reverent. It's almost as if we're learning how to perform surgery, I think, watching Billy work my mother's chest.

My mother sobs softly next to me. After a while her breathing finally slows and quiets, Billy kneeling there the entire time with his hand pressed to my mother's heart, repairing her.

After he gets my mother back into a seated position he stands and walks to the front of the room. As he sits on his carpeted platform he says without ceremony or explanation, "My wife and son are dead. It's why we're here now, and why we weren't here a month ago. My wife Anna was thirty-four. Deepak was three. They drowned in the bathtub. You all know this. The people outside know this. I've been very sad, and shocked, and all the things that people feel when someone they love has died. It's something that happened, that can't be undone. There's no softness in wishing time could go backwards. That if only I'd been home at the time, if only she didn't take a bath, if only Deepak had been spared. *If onlys* drown you too. So we're here to remember Anna and Deepak, and to honor them by opening ourselves to reality, to truth. And the truth is, people stop breathing. Whether or not reincarnation is true, people we know and love cease to exist on this plane, and we go on without them." Billy's voice cracks. A scattering of women blow their noses. Many more wipe their eyes. "Thank you all for being here," he goes on, crying openly. "For joining me to brave the depths of pain, to realize the truth of our essence and make peace with what haunts us all. Namaste."

"Namaste," we say.

Then he gets down to business. He says, "Everyone sit up straight. You want your breath to flow without any obstacles.

Nothing fancy or complicated. Easy, straight, tall. Now inhale on a slow count of ten and hold it for ten. Then let it out for ten. When you're done, breathe normally, no *ujjayi*. No *bandhas*. Just be real with the breath. No trying. No yoga. Just be."

After our breathing exercise it's time to befriend our demons. Billy leads us part of the way, instructing us to travel down into the deepest pit we can imagine—under water, in the pitch blackness, at the bottom of a well. "Whatever's there, just grab it and be there," he says. "This is not about art-directing the perfect setting. Just follow the image. Got it?"

He sets us up in our darknesses facing an empty seat, which he instructs us to fill with the worst aspect of ourselves. When we meet this aspect, we are to allow it to come alive as an entity all its own, whether as an animal, human being or deity of some sort. He tells us that we can do this exercise over and over, all our lives, that there will always be a demon waiting to befriend us. It's reassuring to know we're all screwed up.

We are to gesture for the demon to communicate its deepest need, and then we will offer our demon our warm glowing heart chakra. "There might be a series of mutations," Billy says. "Just allow it all to unfold, like you're watching a movie. No forcing. No censoring. No editing. Just be there as a loving, patient witness. Don't even try to interpret. Just watch and be there with your heart. Everybody clear?"

My mother begins crying again, almost immediately. Then others join her. First it's one other woman, sniffling from somewhere behind me. Then I hear another. Then a man's soft weeping. Soon the whole room is alive with unabashed sobs and I can't help but find my own added to the chorus.

My mind takes me to a soot-stained room with stone walls like the ones in the lobby of my mother's apartment building, modeled to look like an Arthurian castle, empty except for me in there, sitting on a maroon velvet pillow opposite a leather throne with carved wooden armrests. I can't concentrate on my demon at all with this racket. I take a deep breath to calm myself down and that's when she appears.

Gaping at me through puffy, slitty eyes, her upper lip glistening with mucus, bottom lip jutting, sits a little girl in a woolen dress with an anchor stitched to the chest. Her black hair is pulled tight into two high ponytails and her bangs are cut crookedly, a jagged streak of lightning that traverses her forehead well above her eyebrows. She clutches a naked, armless plastic doll, scribbled all over with black magic marker. Her fingernails are bitten to the quick and her body is wrapped tightly in thread. Every time she tries to wriggle free the thread cuts into her skin and thin lines of blood appear. On her feet are a pair of scuffed red patent-leather Mary Janes. I know that she is being punished for cutting her own bangs, for ruining her doll, for scuffing her shoes. I know her father wrapped her in the thread while her mother smoked cigarettes in the closet. I know the little girl wishes she had metal taps nailed to the soles of her shoes, so she could dance.

I ask her what she needs most of all.

When she opens her mouth, a black eel slithers out. The eel swims around her body, starting at her shoes. As it spirals toward her head the thread falls to the floor in wet clumps. The girl stands up, finally freed, and shakes her body out like a rag doll, tiny drops of blood flying off her. She lifts her arms and turns in slow motion like a plastic ballerina in a music box and I see that her spine is covered in bony plates. As she dances the bloody cuts on her arms and legs dry up like a parched desert, leaving scales where skin once was. She elbows the air, kicks her legs in a crazy jig. Her skin begins to glimmer greenly, her mouth launches open and her tongue emerges, forked like a snake's, the color of a bruise. Her eyes turn red as she stares at me, not caring what I think. She is ecstatic. She is a beast. I watch her with my heart glowing gold until she transforms completely and slithers away into the darkness, her pointed tail flicking defiantly behind her. She never said a word.

Her throne dissolves and in its place appears a silvery shimmering vision of a man walking toward me wearing nothing but white pajama bottoms. An invisible cord that stretches from my throat through my glowing heart to my groin pulls taut as he gets closer. My velvet pillow vanishes along with the dungeon, and a stretch of white sand appears, surrounded by a tropical turquoise sea where dolphins leap. The cord pulls me toward him. When I reach him our eyes lock. We press our bodies together. I dig my fingers through his tangle of hair while he presses his hands to my back, which expands and relaxes like never before. My core ignites and our hearts meld into one shining, fiery sun. He kisses me. I gasp audibly and my eyes snap open to see that Billy is staring at me from the stage, and he looks terrified.

"I feel *deeply* changed," my mom says, nestled into the heated leather passenger seat of Billy's car, and then speaks of her plans to begin one-on-one sessions with him right away. "He has a month-long immersion program that sounds absolutely cathartic," she says, beaming at him. She clutches a handful of paper—a brochure, a catalog, a few flyers and postcards. Then she turns to me. "Thank you so much, my darling daughter, for inviting me to this workshop. Did you get anything from it?"

"Mom," I say, feeling uncomfortably adolescent, wishing she'd embrace silence for once, wishing I could figure out if I was dreaming or not when Billy—well, when it seemed like he was *in* my visualization with me. That kiss we shared reverberates through my entire body, leaving me very confused. And bewildered. And horny.

"Well, did you? I am your mother. Am I not allowed to inquire after your spiritual well-being?"

"Yes, Mother. I got something out of it."

"I am glad to hear that, Eve, because I really think this type of thing is good for you. It can really free you up, like I was freed today. Do you know what I saw down there?"

"You don't have to tell me," I say, bracing myself against my mother's fresh self-actualized take on life.

"I saw your grandmother. On the boardwalk in Ventnor," she says. "I know we were supposed to go underground," she says as an aside to Billy, "but she was there on the boardwalk proud as anything, with her purse and her hat. It was so vivid. And you know what? She was so *unhappy.*"

"That's too bad," I say, wondering how Billy could have possibly entered my meditation. No, I'm overreacting. Wishful thinking. He's just too damned hot. That's all it is.

"It's a shame. So sad." She turns to Billy. "I wish my other daughter could have come. This would have been so good for her. She works so hard. And she's divorced, raising a boy on her own. Such a smart, pretty woman. Kine hora poo poo poo."

I press my fist into the seat back behind my mom. What is she doing? Setting Billy up with Jeannie? I wish I could tape her mouth shut.

Then she admonishes me again. "What about you, Eve? What did you see?"

"I'd rather not talk about it," I say, glancing at Billy, who's staring at me again through the rearview, and I could swear he looks tense—scared, really. I look away, out the window, where all I see is Billy anyway, walking toward me, shirtless and barefoot, his tongue flicking like a snake's.

Chapter 15

ou start on the Halloween costumes?" Neil asks. We're in the
kitchen eating dinner.

"I found a box," I say, poking at my salad. I haven't had much
of an appetite since the meditation workshop. That little girl keeps
haunting me, with her snake tongue. And that kiss. That haunts me
too. I can't stop thinking about it. Sometimes I catch myself tilting
my head, closing my eyes and kissing the air. Then I come to and
realize what a fool I am. Especially when I find Chloe staring at me
quizzically, asking, "Mommy, what are you doing?"

"I'm happy to do it," he says, swigging his beer.

"Hers is basically done," I say. "As long as she agrees to wear her
cowboy boots."

"CowGIRL boots," Chloe corrects me.

"Cow*girl* boots," I repeat. "I keep saying that, don't I?"

"Mommy," she scolds, her hair dragging through the grated
parmesan on her plate.

"So you'll wear them?" I ask.

"Sure!" she pipes, bright as ever, oblivious to the strain between
her father and me.

"Better start his tomorrow," Neil says. It sounds like a warning.

"I will," I say. It sounds defensive.

"I said I'd be happy to do it," he says.

"Guys, be nice," Chloe says, refereeing.

Sam perches with one knee on his chair, bouncing up and down on the ball of his standing foot and chewing way too big a bite of ravioli. "I fink I wannoo ee a howeranger," he manages, spraying cheese crumbs out of his mouth and laughing at how funny he thinks he is.

"You're going to be a robot," Neil and I bark in tandem, which makes both kids laugh and show even more of the half-chewed contents of their mouths. I look at Neil, but he is not amused.

For the remainder of the weekend I spend hours at the sink washing dishes that could easily fit into the dishwasher. Compelled by a mixture of desire, information greed and neurotic fear, I read everything I can about Billy and Anna Lisko online, wading through hostile chatrooms, snarky and speculative blog posts and volatile, accusatory comment threads until I feel dirty and sullied. People out there are having a grand time resurrecting Richard Dorian Sr. and placing his ghost at the scene of the crime—LOL! Or concocting stories of hot-tub three-ways gone wrong, starring the Dorian brothers and Anna. This is the first bit of information linking Rick to Anna. One commenter who I imagine as a pimply kid with carpal tunnel from jerking off all day is certain that Anna had it coming for being such a 'hot slut'—that Billy should have drowned her in the toilet—LMFAO!!!! A subsequent commenter adds, "yea. that way the kid woulda lived lol." I can't tear myself away.

Like Justicia, Anna came from a wealthy family. Instead of a chain of fancy department stores, Anna's father made his fortune in cable TV. She was from Gladwyne, which I learn is the twelfth richest suburb in the country. This explains how an acupuncturist and a life coach could afford a complete home remodel. I'd been wondering about that too.

An article from a psychology website theorizes the extent of emotional damage abuse-sufferers face, and cites the Dorian boys as prime examples, despite no reports that the boys themselves were abused by their father. It goes on to document their emotionally fueled behavior in their late teen years, including a fire that Billy set at his high school which he got suspended for, and a week Rick went missing with his fourteen year-old girlfriend when Rick was seventeen, just two years after Justicia's murder. Upon their return, Rick admitted to flying the girl to Hawaii, using money they had stolen from the girl's parents, who did not press charges. There were multiple mentions of drugs—pot mostly, and hallucinogens—underage drinking and sexual activity, like the time when Billy was fifteen and it was revealed that he had been having repeated sexual relations with his nineteen-year-old cousin.

Another post made connections between Justicia Dorian and Anna Lisko. It reported that both women were beautiful, headstrong, opinionated, independent and from well-to-do families. It alleged that their strength and wealth triggered feelings of deep insecurity and inadequacy in both Richard Sr. and Billy, both men known to be temperamental. The article mentioned Billy's motorcycle accident and the well-documented fist-fights during college that led to his eventual expulsion from Temple University for punching a professor. The author of the article did everything but outright accuse Billy of murdering Anna and Deepak.

I pore over information that is none of my business, and when I break to pee I stare at his house through my bathroom window, and by nightfall, a darkness so impermeable settles over me that I leave the laptop and head outside. I walk along Medford to Morris Road, down Wynnewood Road and into Ardmore along Spring Avenue, where the houses shrink into shabby twins with aluminum siding, crumbling sidewalks and patchy lawns, but still manage to decorate the curbs with red and yellow Hummers. I walk for miles, as if I can unknow everything I've learned, shed the information like dog hair. Or snake skin. Fondling my cell phone in my pocket, I yank it out and dial the police station. I have the number memorized.

"Hi, this is Eve Myer. I was wondering what the update is on the Anna Lisko case. I live next door to them—to Billy Dorian. I've called before and spoken to Detective Bryant."

After five minutes on hold, Detective Bryant comes to the phone. "Thank you for your patience, Mrs. Myer," she says in her thick Philly accent, heavy on the Rs and short As, eating the Os along the way. "What can I do for you?"

"I was just wondering if you're going to arrest me. There are people out there who think I had something to do with this. And I never hear from you. It's like I keep expecting you to show up at my house with handcuffs, but the doorbell never rings. So if I'm not a suspect I wish you'd just tell me so I can stop, you know, like, waiting for the phone to ring." This is a new low in the blossoming of my second adolescence. Waiting to get a call from the police? I would laugh if I weren't so nervous.

"Mrs. Myer, we cleared your name over a week ago," Detective Bryant says. "You can stop waiting by the phone now, dear."

"What? How? I mean that's great, but—"

"You were on the phone with a Mrs. Marilyn Shankin from roundabout nine till eleven the night of the ninth and then again early on the morning of the tenth?"

I'd totally forgotten about that. "My mom," I say. "We talk a lot. She's worried about a mole on her arm. Thinks it's cancer. She's at that age I guess."

"I see. Well, it's very good news to hear you have a close relationship with your mother."

"It's great," I lie. My mother ranting and raving for two straight hours about her real and fictional medical ailments does not a close relationship make.

"Anything else?" I ask.

"We found Ms. Lisko's diary."

"Oh," I say softly.

"She thought very highly of you," Detective Bryant says.

"Wow," I say.

"Feels good, doesn't it, Mrs. Myer."

"It does," I say. Then, "So does this mean I can have my writing back? It's scraps of paper that Officer Vale took. That is, if it's not needed anymore."

"You sure can, Mrs. Myer," she says, bored. Maybe slightly amused. "You want to come by tonight?"

"Oh, not tonight," I say, surprised by the immediacy of her invitation. "Maybe tomorrow? And, um, is Billy really being considered a suspect? Because there is a lot of speculation online and it's really unfair, you know, if he's innocent, which I think he is, because I find him to be an upstanding citizen, not to mention the fact that he wasn't even there. And I go on the record with that."

"Duly noted, Mrs. Myer."

"Good. Thank you. So is there any way to stop these people from slandering him? Is there even any evidence that this whole thing wasn't just a tragic accident?"

"Mrs. Myer, why don't you come by the station tomorrow. Pick up your things. We've got copies on file. As far as whether it was intentional or accidental, we're still waiting for the autopsy report. That's the most I can tell you for the time being. And as far as Mr. Dorian's name being slandered, I'd say call a lawyer, but you know how that goes."

"It goes *ka-ching*," I say, enjoying our little chat, now that I'm officially not a murder suspect. And yet, there was something glamorous about being doubted.

"That's right, Mrs. Myer. It's cost-prohibitive. I'd suggest you go off-line for a while. Stay away from common stressors. There's so much hatred being spewed on the Internet these days. It's just like road rage."

"I guess," I say. "Thanks, Detective."

"You're welcome, Mrs. Myer. Good night now."

One day when Neil takes the kids out for soft pretzels I spy on Billy alone in his house from my dining room into his living room. At first I think he's practicing Tai Chi but then I realize he's dancing. To a slowish song. Maybe medium tempo. He sways and twirls, juts his hips. Jumps in the air with his hands overhead. Undulates to the beat. I could see him onstage in an arena—a glittery sexed-up rock star. Jim Morrison meets Mick Jagger. All he's wearing is a pair of low-slung track pants. No shirt. My breath snags as I watch him move. Broad shoulders, flat belly, narrow hips. I allow my eyes to roam his body, collecting him in pieces—the trail of dark hair leading from his belly button to his crotch, the hair in his armpits, small pink nipples, the hair, bouncing, matted, tangled. As if he's just rolled out of bed after a week of hibernation. The various perfectly proportioned slopes traversing his body—where his ass swells from the small of his back. His chest, triceps, those twin crescents dividing his hips from his belly. What are those called? A quick Google reveals the answer—*Adonis belt*. The moving picture before me lights a fire in the pit of my belly. When he finally collapses onto his sofa and stares into space, I see that he's crying. I steal upstairs and climb into bed, burrowing under the covers with my vibrator, which is losing battery power. When it finally dies I finish myself off with my hand. I picture Billy, rumpled, inviting, half naked—and let the fantasy unfold like I did in the workshop.

Without a word Billy takes my hand in his Mount Airy waiting room and leads me outside, through a secret door to the privacy wall in his backyard where sunlight streams down upon us. He takes my face in his hands, slowly leans in to kiss me but stops himself short. Our eyes remain open, gazing. He grips my wrists in his hands, lifts them out to the sides, presses my body back into the Spanish moss cascading down the wall. The moss wraps around my wrists, restraining me under his command. He unbuttons my jeans, slides them to my ankles, caresses my legs and hips as he makes his way to stand again. The cascading green claims my shirt, sucks it off my body and into the wall. I stand naked and bound. I can feel the weight of his body pressing against mine—his belly, chest and thighs. He reaches between my legs and rubs slow circles in exactly the right place as he gazes at me. He is a virtuoso with those practiced fingers of his, so sensitive to what lies beneath them.

I feel his breath on my face.

His cock presses against my thigh through his jeans. I want to reach down and stroke it but my wrists are bound. I kick my jeans off my feet, lift my legs and wrap them around his waist, pulling him to me but he pulls away and the vines curl around my ankles, restraining them too. "Not today," he says.

I beg him with my eyes.

"You're greedy, aren't you?" he whispers.

"Yes," I confess.

"Eve," he says, his voice a hoarse whisper. His cock presses a dent into my thigh, even through the fabric.

"Please," I plead.

"You know you can't fuck me. It's against the rules."

"Fuck the rules," I say.

"I hate rules too," he says, and his voice betrays a desire that could swallow us both.

His fingers circle more rapidly, sweeping inside me and then flicking that ridge of pulsating weakness.

"Fuck me," I say. The weight of his body, the heat emanating from his chest, his face, is narcotic.

"Eve," he says.

"Please," I say.

"Eve," he says. Breathing harder.

"Billy."

He tilts his head, parts his lips. Leans in to me. Our mouths connect. Lips on fire. Tongues darting. He unzips his fly, frees his erection, presses it into my thigh. I wrench against the vines to free my hands, my legs as I struggle to look at it. He presses harder against me, grinds into my body so that it jams against the wall.

He pulls away. I struggle toward him for more. *"Please,"* I say.

"Wait for me," he says, breath heavy, eyes blazing. There's wetness on my thigh. A drop.

"I promise..." His fingers return to me. I tremble under his expert touch. My hands and feet grow icy as the fire collects in my center and I finally, breathlessly explode.

Before my next visit I drive to CVS and wander the aisles cloaked in a desirous stupor, unsure of what exactly I've come for. A potion, lotion or product, something magical that will cast me out of domesticity and into the realm of possibility, of freedom. I pass a jumbled display of jauntily colored reading glasses. I pass the romance novels, magazines and Sudoku puzzles. A mother haggles with her toddler over a Little Mermaid coloring book in the middle of the aisle and I have to nearly step over them to get by. I pass the prescription counter where a few people sit like giant tumors on the vomit-colored seats, looking as though they've been waiting there since the dawn of time. Does anyone really come here to buy cigars, pork rinds and potato Stix? I've traversed all the aisles twice, listening on my cell to Jeannie's latest take on the drowning. "Did you hear that Billy got expelled from Temple?" she says. "Punched a professor."

"So you don't think it was an accident anymore?" I say, refusing to believe that Billy Dorian, with his Taoism and eastern healing modalities, could stoop to drowning his wife and baby.

"It probably was. The whole thing's just getting blown out of proportion. Modern society is the devil. He is cute though," she concurs.

"Yeah," I sigh. "You know mom was talking you up to him. I think she wants to set you guys up." An old lady scowls at me in the First Aid aisle where she's clutching an ACE Bandage, and I start laughing. Screw her.

When we hang up I keep browsing, past the shoe inserts, Slim-Fast, jumbo containers of berry-flavored Tums and grapefruit body wash. All the while I imagine getting fucked by Billy from behind in his waiting room in Mount Airy. In the hair care aisle, after considering about fifteen different products, I finally settle on a jar of molding paste that promises to leave my hair beach-scented and artfully mussed. At the counter I ask for an eight-pack of C batteries.

Back at home I dress carefully in an old pair of khakis and a faded tank top with a bleach-stained cardigan. Nothing dressy. Padded bra. Carefully applied foundation, blush, sheer lip gloss, hair washed and carefully arranged with glittery globs of eighteen-dollar product. Neil sticks his head in the bathroom on his way to iron his work shirt. "Going somewhere special?" he asks.

My mouth pops open as I turn to look at him, flustered for what to say. I can feel the gel hardening on my fingertips.

"You look nice," he says, considering my existence, and turns away.

"Thank you," I say, as the ironing board screams open on its rusty hinges. It's the nicest exchange we've had in months.

Soon enough I'm perched on the leather sofa in the waiting room. I take a deep breath to slow my heart and touch my hair. The ends have crisped into wavy little snakes.

Billy slides the pocket door open, stands there, looks into my eyes.

He tells me, "I have to talk to you." It comes out like a confession and I can feel him waiting for my response.

I open my mouth to respond but he's gazing at me so intently that the floor steals my gaze.

Chapter 16

I look across the driveway into his house. The SUV is gone. I can see Billy in his living room, sitting on the floor in lotus position, meditating in front of a candle. He's been there for over an hour. I can't sleep, so I've been checking on him.

Our conversation at his office went like this—

Billy: Did you notice anything strange about your visualization?

Me: Like what?

Billy: Well, like—like, I know this sounds really weird, but was I in it by any chance?

Me: Uh…

Billy: It's okay, Eve. It's okay, don't tell me. It's none of my business. I'm sorry. But can you tell me if there was a beach?

Me: You were there! I knew it!

Billy: Was I wearing white pants?

Me: Yes!

Billy: No shirt?

Me: Yes.

Billy: And did we—kiss?

Me: Yes.

Billy: How did this—

Me: This is so fucked up.

Billy: I didn't mean to. I mean, I didn't even know I could—unless you—

Me: Nooo. I had nothing to do with it.

Billy: So you mean, I, like, entered your visualization?

Me: I think so.

Billy: Or did you summon me into it?

Me: I don't do much summoning as far as I know.

Billy: Jesus.

Me: Yeah.

Billy: Wow.

Me: I know.

Finally I crawl into bed and take some deep breaths.

Neil mumbles, "What time is it?"

"Three-thirty," I whisper.

"Jesus," he says.

I touch myself to the movie clip in my mind of Billy and me kissing, but no relief comes. I slide my finger inside myself and then flick it across my clitoris, thinking about how Billy somehow entered my head space, pulled me close and kissed me. For a minute I feel hot. Aroused. But the fantasy spits and sputters. I can't keep it going, maybe because the whole situation is so entirely weird. And I can't use batteries now. They'll wake Neil. I work myself over with my fingers until I just feel achy and empty and raw, and then fall into a fitful, unsatisfying sleep.

When I wake a couple hours later, I'm dopey with exhaustion and my heart is pounding with anxiety. I can hear little Deepak shrieking in the yard. Oh no. I can't. Deepak's dead. I realize this and my heart sinks. Tears come again, stinging my eyes. Too much sadness, I think.

I make a batch of fudge. Leave it at Billy's door while Neil sleeps. That afternoon while I'm in the basement hot gluing bottle tops to a cardboard box, the phone rings. My heart leaps into my throat, my nerves are so raw.

"Eve?" she slurs.

"Mom? Are you drunk?"

"Eve, I think I had a little shtroke."

"When?"

"Lasht night."

"And you waited until now to call me? What happened?"

"I was tshalking to Yoyo on the phone lasht night and I felt this chingle on my right sheek and now the left shide of my faish is drooping and my left arm is weak. Oh Eve, my faish looksh sherrible."

"Oh Mom," I say tenderly, and realize I mean it. It turns out I love this woman, no matter how much Vaseline she smears on her face, no matter how many offensive, inappropriate, insulting, Tourette's-like proclamations she blurts.

"Anyway, I took shum Bufferin and went to bed. Do you think you can call your mother-in-law and then come over? I don't want to be alone."

"You don't want me to call Jeannie?"

"Oh no, she'll jusht worry."

"She's a nurse, Mom."

"Maybe we can call her when you get here," she suggests. "Please come."

We hang up and I promptly break down into tears, and scream for Neil who's upstairs carving a jack-o-lantern with the kids. He comes to the top of the stairs, his hands covered with orange slime. I tell him the news, and he rinses his hands and hugs me, then starts packing a backpack for the kids. I start filling a totebag with leftovers, because in my dawning shock, my mother's instructions sound logical and reasonable and she never has any food, save for salad dressing and mango juice. We'll just *not* call my ER nurse sister, hang out at my mom's and talk to my mother-in-law on the phone, who's a retired dialysis nurse in Kutztown. Who said anything about a hospital?

It takes forever to get everyone ready. Getting out the door is like trudging through creamed honey. My mom calls my cell while we're in the car. "You know, why don't you call Viola now? Don't bother coming over. It'sh okay. I'll be fine."

I hang up and decide that *maybe* going against my mother's wishes and calling my sister is actually a good idea. "Mom had a stroke," I text her.

Jeannie is brilliant. She texts back, "Take her to the hospital." Why hadn't I thought of this before? Maybe because I don't have an MSN from The University of Pennsylvania. It turns out that when you have a stroke you need to go to the hospital *right away*.

I call my mother back.

"We're taking you to the hospital. Jeannie will meet us there."

"You called her?" she says, crestfallen.

"A stroke is a *medical emergency*, Mother," I hiss.

"Okay," she says, defeated. "Can you bring me something to hold up the shide of my faish?"

"How about some Scotch tape?"

"Perfect," she says.

"It won't stick to the Vaseline though."

"Very funny."

"Listen, maybe I should just call 911 for you?"

"Oh no. I don't want the neighborsh peering out their doors."

Again, this sounds reasonable. It's none of their business. Let's not cause a scene. It's only a shlight shtroke.

"Okay, we'll be over soon," I say.

My adorable stroked-out mom is ambling around her apartment at low speed, slurring, "I managed to brush my teeth. Can you believe that?" She's not nearly as droopy as I'd anticipated. Sam takes one look at her and runs into her bedroom to watch The Cartoon Network.

My mom whispers to me how much money she's got in her bank account, waving her checkbook in my face, and shows me the bills that need to get paid but tells me she's having trouble writing since she's left-handed. She has trouble buttoning her coat because it's too tight and she's just had a stroke and keeps dropping her keys. She says, "Aren't I fat?" and lets the coat fall to the floor. "I didn't want to wear the green one anyway," she announces, and shuffles out of the kitchen. Neil and I look at each other and can't help but laugh through our mild terror.

Chloe says, clutching her stuffed puppy, "Why is she acting so silly, Mommy?"

"It's like she's herself, but magnified," I remark and we nearly trip over ourselves getting my mother and her pills and her cell phone and her library book and her giant cataract sunglasses packed up. We nearly leave Sam behind until Neil recalls that we have a son.

On the way to the hospital, I quiz my mom on everyone's birthday, as well as the current president and today's date. This stroke did not affect her memory. She announces every one correctly, if slurringly.

Neil drops us off at the emergency room and goes to park. My mother tells the nice lady at the desk, "I think I'm having a shlight shtroke." She manages to sign over her life on the forms, very well I may add, considering she's lost a lot of mobility in that left arm of hers, and then mutters something about *schvartzas*, which I, filled with horror, demand that she cease because the nice lady at the desk is black. Then I crack up because I'm exhausted and cannot believe I'm related to this racist clown.

We speed through triage with the help of Alan, a lovely nurse with a bad toupee. While I peel the kids off the floor, Alan insists that my mother be wheeled to a bed which she eventually agrees is a good idea. When the doctor arrives and touches my mother's face, asking if she can feel his fingers, she tells him with doe eyes, "I can feel everything and it feels very nice." This, after asking him if he's old enough to have even completed medical school. I shiver, seeing myself in her coy ways. The way I am with Billy. I could vomit from embarrassment.

Jeannie arrives as the lady in the bed to our right, a witchy bag of bones with an explosion of gray hair and crusty feet, starts her lunchtime show. She shouts for help. Her pleas go ignored and we learn that this is because she's insane. When no aid arrives she gets out of her bed, spilling tea, falling out of her gown, clutching God knows what to her sunken chest. Wide-eyed with terror, she peers into our little antiseptic beeping cove where my mother lies prone (so her head can receive as much blood as possible). The shrunken old woman looks pleadingly into my eyes—why me?—and says, "Can you help me?"

I swallow, clutching Chloe's shoulders while Sam watches in horror. I look to Jeannie for support but she's jabbing at her phone, wildly ignoring my time of need. "What?" she says, looking at me. "I have to let Larry know what's going on."

"You suck," I say.

"Please help me," the old lady says, taking a step closer. "I want to swim with the dolphins!"

The twelve-year-old doctor thankfully witnesses the commotion and escorts the old lady back to her bed just as I'm about to tell her she's going to need to fly to the Caribbean, or Hawaii.

Neil joins us as the lady pulls out a stash of cigarettes and lights up. The cigarettes get confiscated, the nurses roll their eyes from behind their computers and my family's faces shine with a mixture of mirth and wonder. *This is the best stroke ever!*

I can't help but wonder how Billy would handle the situation with the cigarette lady. With my mom. My mother would probably try to mount him. I keep thinking I see him here, out of the corner of my eye.

Jeannie continues to ignore the commotion—she's seen it all already—while our mother pleads with us to open the curtain so she can see the show. Jeannie leans over and explains for the third time that my mother must not lift her head. "Mom, it's nothing important," she says. "Just focus on relaxing."

A few minutes later the old woman whips out her second, hidden stash of smokes from where I can only imagine, and lights up again. We howl with laughter. Even Jeannie smiles, despite her jadedness.

This time there are words. "Hey jerkoff!" the old lady calls to Jim, another nurse on duty. "Kiss my blow-hole!" She bends over and her gown splits as she moons him. Sam's jaw drops. I slap a hand across Chloe's eyes as the old lady pulls her wrinked ass cheeks apart so we can all get a look at her grizzled *blow-hole*. "Go get your own cigarettes!" she spits when she stands back up, readjusting herself like a windblown queen.

"I don't smoke, ma'am," Jim responds calmly, staring into his computer screen and typing furiously.

"That's what I thought," she mutters, as if his non-smoking status betrays a lack of character she obviously possesses in spades. Then, "When am I getting my own room?"

"That's what I want to know," he says, without hiding his disdain. "I'm trying to find out right now."

Jeannie says, "Thank God," when they finally take her away, but the rest of us are sad. I'm heartened to know the kids will have something fun to discuss with their friends at school.

After another hour or so, my mother gets relocated to her own room since the tests have determined that her stroke wasn't slight, but a full-on regular-sized stroke. The petite neurologist arrives soon after and reports the effects to be moderate to medium. Jeannie says, "Mom, do you have any idea how lucky you are? And how stupid you were? This could have been so much worse." But when the doctor ominously suggests that my mother not live alone for the time being, Jeannie whips her phone out again, avoiding all eye contact.

My mother responds to the news with, "Hey, you can all move in with me!" like it's a party. I know she loves her practically empty one bedroom apartment with its king-sized bed, but I don't think our family of four will fit there comfortably. My brother Larry is too rural for my mom's metropolitan tastes, Jeannie's house is out of the question since she's never home and she's such a slob. That leaves us.

Neil and I look at each other and sigh. "What do you want me to bring from your house, Mom?" I ask her. "We'll set up the guest room for you."

Chapter 17

I have no idea how to take care of a sick septuagenarian, and Jeannie is no help. Luckily it turns out it's a lot like caring for a kindergartener. Bathing and feeding her is the worst, most disturbing part, but she's mostly able and I refuse to scrub her below the waist. I sort her pills, set up her room, and even help her with her physical therapy exercises when Chloe and Sam haven't made off with her foam ball and other curious medical gadgets.

The night of Halloween, Neil and I sit on the family room floor, stupid with exhaustion, with two large Tupperware containers and a plastic jack-o-lantern bucket, separating the chocolate from the rest of the loot so we can freeze it until next October and give it right back to the neighborhood. My mom and the kids are finally asleep. Sam would have fallen asleep in his costume if we didn't intervene. I can't imagine he would have been too comfortable sleeping in a box. But such is the way of the long trudge door to door followed by the requisite sugar overdose.

"I feel like we haven't talked in so long," I say, plucking three Kit-Kats and a miniature Milky Way Dark from the plastic pumpkin and placing them into the Tupperware container.

"Yeah," Neil says. He swipes the Milky Way, unwraps it and

pops it into his mouth. "I've just been... I don't know... It's all been so—"

"I know," I say. "It's okay."

Neil shakes his head as if nothing is okay and we divide in silence for a while.

"So did you ever call the police?" I ask.

"Yeah. Last week," he says.

"What'd they say?"

"They were fine about it. Said that kind of thing happens all the time. Said to sit tight, there'd be more information soon."

"Well that's good news."

"Yeah."

I yawn. "Billy's just really nice. It doesn't fit that he did it. I don't want to incriminate anyone."

"Eve," Neil says after a few moments of silent sorting. "Have you done anything with Billy?"

"What?" I ask. "Are you serious? How can you even think that?"

"Oh well, let's see. You've so much as said you're attracted to him. You see him once a week in his office where he does God knows what to you. You can't stop bringing him baked goods. How could I possibly think something was going on between you two?"

"I have not done anything with Billy," I say.

"Good," he says.

"I'm not like that," I add meanly.

"Good," he says again, not biting.

"Do you believe me?" I ask, after a minute or two.

He sighs. "Yeah. I guess I do."

"Convincing," I say.

We sort in silence for a while longer.

"Do you think we should have sex?" I finally blurt.

"Are you trying to divert my attention?"

"Yes. And no. Forget it."

"You want to?" he asks, wary.

"Should we finish this first?"

"I think we should have sex," he says, moving to stand up. "It's only been, what, like six months?"

After shoving the rest of the candy into a high kitchen cabinet we're in our room, standing on opposite sides of the bed, stripping. My husband's hips used to be so narrow, the kind of hips I always wanted—prepubescent, boyish. Now they glow swollen and white against the dark patch between them. I turn off the light, and the streetlight outside casts a bluish glow in the room. Neil peels the covers back. He is already hard.

We slide into bed. I ponder his penis. Penises used to surprise me with their purple wormy strangeness. But I know Neil's so well now, with its freckle toward the base, the slight curve it makes, as if it's pointing at the tiny chocolate mole on his soft belly. I lay on my side and pet his erection. The delicate skin shifts when I stroke it. He sighs his approval.

I pet it a few more times, and when he tells me it feels good I say, "No talking."

Without warning I leave the bed and walk into the bathroom, leaving Neil momentarily alone with his engorged penis. But I already know I will need help with this venture.

"Everything okay?" he calls.

"It's fine. I'll be right there." The K-Y in my vanity drawer is older than Sam but it still does the job. I flip the cap open, squeeze out a blob and carry it back to bed, a glistening pet.

He lays there in the semi-dark with his hands behind his head. Then he takes one of his hands and pulls on his balls. I look at his chest and belly, pale and bloated, silvery hairs sprouting from around each rosy nipple. My body takes over, straddling him and swirling the K-Y on the head of his penis as he shifts approvingly: hips rise, hand flips the erection toward the ceiling and slides it inside. Face descends to his neck where it will remain. Pelvises press tight to one another. Hips circle clockwise, crotch mashed against crotch, going round and round until the friction is enough to cause an orgasm. His neck is wet. I've drooled.

Then it's his turn. Up and down I go. He moans. Tilts his head back, squeezes his eyes shut. His mouth opens. I don't have to look behind me to know that his feet clench and his toes curl. Then the held breath. Then the "Oh God," then the satisfied swallow and sigh. He opens his eyes, looks at me with heavy-lidded gratitude and a hint of shame, runs his palm down the side of my torso almost carelessly, the sensation of my skin under his touch long forgotten.

"Good stuff," he says and reaches behind his pillow for his boxers.

I nod, take the underwear and begin the work of wiping up.

"Eve, it'll be okay," he says as I return to bed from the bathroom.

"What will?"

"Everything."

I nestle against him, tucking my hand in his armpit, and fall instantly asleep.

Chapter 18

ey," Billy says, greeting me in the examining room doorway, his arm leaning up against the jamb in a pose that appears casual but seems tinged around the edges with discomfort. Maybe it's his eyes. They dart around the room, never quite landing, like a hummingbird.

I catch his eyes flickering up and down my body, taking in my baggy sweatpants and oversized T-shirt, cloaked by a long hoodie. He doesn't look at me lasciviously, but impulsively, intuitively. In a way that a better woman might mind, in a way she might not even notice.

I place my mat, a scroll of recycled rubber, in the corner, feeling the red rise to the top of my head. I've already registered his attire for the day—inky Levi's and a faded long sleeved shirt that clings to his arms just enough to accentuate their definition.

I realize that I no longer know where to look either. I'm afraid if I look into his eyes he will see how I've fallen for him, see what I know, but if I look away he will think I suspect him. I decide that all I can do is cling to some sense of contrived normalcy.

"I'm glad you remembered your mat," he says. His answering service left a message asking if I wouldn't mind coming prepared to do yoga for my next appointment, to which my response was panic.

I smile weakly. "Om shanti," I say.

"Listen, don't worry. I'm not here to judge your practice," he says. "I'm not going to make you do anything too straining. I just want to get a sense of what poses hurt, which ones don't affect the pain, and see how we can help you modify."

"Oh, okay. Sure," I say, feeling unsure of exactly everything, but ready to tango. From the looks of it, our song will be 'Let's pretend nothing weird and slightly paranormal ever happened between us.'

"Why don't you set up," he says. "Warm up, and then do a couple surya namaskars. Those pretty much cover the gamut, right?"

I nod, impressed by his esoteric vocab. "Do you practice?"

"I've done a little. So many studios just bastardize it though, you know? Everyone's got to put their hand in. Trademark it. Claim ownership. Power yoga. Bikram. It's such a racket. So just meditation for now. That's the goal anyway, right?"

"I wish I had more time for meditation, but the kids," I explain. "Does staring at a wall count?"

"Why not?" he allows. "Can you do it for twenty minutes at a time?"

Only if it's made of glass, I think, but what I say is still true, if a bit coy. "Only if I stopped coming here."

"We wouldn't want you to do that," he says, looking from me to his hands and back again.

We share a shy smile that lasts a few moments longer than seems professional.

To break the spell I hop off the table and snap my mat open in the middle of the examining room, my heart clanging in my ears.

Finally I shrug the sweatshirt off my shoulders and drop it to the floor beside me. The hairs on my arms rise inside my shirt-sleeves and I shiver. I constrict my throat and begin the long slow inhales and exhales of Ujjayi breathing. I can feel his eyes on me, but I methodically go about my task in the name of spinal health and alternative therapy and not jumping out of my skin. Plus, I need the warmth that the movement will provide.

It makes sense really. This is my sport, so to speak, and Billy is a sort of sports doctor. The trouble is, the "sport" of yoga includes warm-up poses like cat and cow, where, while on your hands and knees, you arch your back and stick out your butt, widening your sitting bones to kingdom come till your rear end puffs out to twice its normal size. It's about as flattering as a broken nose.

But I do it. I have to warm up my spine and if I go half-assed he'll probably think I'm a terrible yogi who deserves to be in constant pain. And anyway, he positions himself so that my butt is not in his face. He's being a gentleman.

Standing in a deep forward fold, I continue my warm-up, extending my spine, and on each exhale I fold again, spreading my sitting bones to stretch my hamstrings. "Do you have any music?" I ask suddenly, my head hanging down between my knees. Who am I kidding? It's impossible not to go bananas. In a yoga class, when you're one of a dozen or so students contorted this way, it's no biggie. But here, alone, in front of Billy, it's like practicing naked.

"You want music? I'll go put some on. Good idea." He nearly leaps out of the room. While he's gone, I think, *Slightly unstable back pain patient takes up with her mysterious witch doctor, embarking on an affair that strains the confines of the doctor's healing room.* I will write it down after this appointment, on a real page in a real notebook, as soon as I buy one. Right after I finally show up at the police station to claim my scraps of moody story ideas.

Lilting strings of a classical guitar begin to fill the room. It's not standard yoga music, not that I'd expect anything standard from Billy. When I press myself into downward dog, he walks toward me, scrutinizing. I claw my fingertips into my mat and lengthen my body as long as I can, to show him I know my way around *adhomuka sva-nasana*. From down dog, it's into plank, then chaturanga, cobra and back to down dog. I wince in pain from the transition from cobra to down dog and find I cannot straighten my legs.

"Right there," Billy says. "You need to slow down. Neutralize your spine between extension and flexion."

He gets on the floor beside me and elongates his frame into plank pose. "Let's try something," he says. His plank is flawless and he lowers himself into chaturanga like he's done it a million times. His triceps contract and I want to cup them in my palm. "I think if you cheat your pelvis a little, tilt it more than feels normal, you can avoid that pinching," he says. "Pull your belly button towards your spine. Create some space in there."

"Okay."

"Let me see you do it." I position my body into plank pose. Billy's hands wrap around my hips and he tucks my pelvis. "Yeah, like that. Now go down."

I descend. My arms shake more than they have in months. My form is terrible.

"Easy. Shoulders back and down. Good. Good."

I make it down to my mat in one piece.

"Now the tiniest baby cobra. Good. No more than that. Keep tucking your tailbone."

My arms are shaking. I forget to breathe. I'm sure he can see my cellulite.

"Excellent," he declares, taking a deep breath. "You have a beautiful practice."

I sit back on my heels and look up at him. "That's all you need?" I squeak, feeling more exposed than an X-ray, and glowing just as brightly from his compliment.

"Why, you want to show me more?" he says, raising his eyebrows in a way that makes me think we are not discussing yoga at all.

"I just thought you'd want to see twists," I explain, feeling like a small animal about to hop into a steel trap. "I get a lot of tightness during twists. And warrior one."

He crosses one arm over his chest and cups his chin with the other. His breathing sounds strained. "You sure it's not too much for you?" he asks.

"It's fine," I say, "Or not. Whatever you think."

"Okay, yeah. Show me a twist," he says, and I almost expect him to add, *and hurry it up.*

I lie back on my mat and let my bent knees fall to the right, keeping my torso planted and feel the familiar pain, possibly good, possibly bad, envelop my postural muscles. Billy crouches to me then. He reaches under my torso then and palpates. "Hm."

"Ow. What?" I try to keep my face from contorting. I'm starting to sweat. I can feel the bloom of wetness on my upper lip.

"It's really tight. I don't like that."

"What does that mean?"

"It means I want you to hold off on the deep twisting. Only go as far as you can before it feels tight. Keep the stretch in the upper back. Do you understand?" He lowers his head and shakes it as if he's disgusted.

"What?" I ask.

"Yoga," he says.

"Didn't Anna practice yoga?" I know I shouldn't have said it before the question leaves my mouth. "I'm sorry. I didn't mean to—"

Billy sighs. Rubs his eyes. Says nothing at first. Then, "She was a yoga junkie," he admits. "But she managed not to get hurt."

My eyebrows shoot up.

"Well—" he corrects, and his eyes fill.

"I miss her," I say.

"Me too," he says.

I make a move to stand up but Billy puts a gently restraining hand on my shoulder.

"Why don't you stay here. Do you mind?"

"No, not at all."

"I like a change in perspective, you know? It's good to do it on the floor once in a while."

I gulp, and look away from him.

I lay back and he wraps his hands under me, getting to work massaging my lumbar muscles. "How are you feeling now?" he asks, and I allow my eyes to meet his for a fleeting moment.

I can't tell him that I feel desirous, turned on, freaked out. "A little weird," I finally admit.

"Weird? Why?" he says with a concern that brings out my maternal side. I want to reach out and stroke his face. Let him know he's doing just fine.

"I've never had an appointment like this before," I say.

"That's why they call it *alternative* therapy," he says, the corner of his mouth turning a smile.

We're quiet for a few moments and in that quiet the air grows heavy with a heart-pounding intimacy I haven't felt in years. I close my eyes and concentrate on the feeling of his hands on my skin, those fingers of his working, focusing, devoted in these precious moments only to me. I break the silence only to groan with pleasure from his fingers pressing into a knot of muscle. Billy doesn't say anything. He just continues kneading my flesh. I allow myself to melt into Billy's skillful hands, allowing them to explore as deeply as they care to go.

Then—"Oh my God," I gasp, when he finds a fresh knot.

"I want to do an adjustment," he says, his voice suddenly clipped. He leans over and embraces me, his face inches from mine, but his eyes are focused on the floor. His fingers splay flat against my spine. "Inhale," he commands and I do, while he lifts my torso off the mat. "And exhale," he says, pressing me into the floor with force.

"How's that?" he asks.

"I don't know," I say, wriggling a bit to feel the effects of his handiwork.

Billy nods and smoothes his hands down his thighs. I steal a glance at him and see a layer of sweat beading on his brow, above his scar. His breath escapes in ragged gasps. "Okay," he says, to indicate that our time is up.

I cover my face with my hands to hide my disappointment that it's over.

"What, not enough for you?" he says, holding out his hand to help me up.

"It's never enough," I whisper, and place my hand in his.

Chapter 19

Y ou don't look nearly as fat as you did last month," she says, reclining on the sofa in the family room, leafing through an old issue of *Lucky*, queen of the castle.

"Would you stop," I say, pulling my hoodie tight around my middle. I've just returned from yoga and am starting to shiver from the layer of cold sweat clinging to me.

She scrutinizes me. "Maybe a little fuller in the face," she says. Her throat and face gleam with Vaseline. A few strands of her reddish hair stick to it like insect legs on fly paper.

"No need to say any of that out loud, Mother."

"So do I get a kiss?" she asks.

I grip her shoulders and carefully pull myself toward her glistening cheek to offer her an air kiss. You could hardly tell she just had a stroke. She's doing great, but her left hand is still weak.

Her whole face sags in disappointment. "You know, I'm not going to be here forever," she warns.

"It feels like forever," I say.

She glares at me, then bursts into laughter, which I join her for.

"Where's Neil?" I say.

"In the basement watching *Fairytopia* with the princess. But please don't join them. Stay with me," she mewls. Then, "I am so thirsty."

I head to the kitchen, make her a glass of tap water with lemon and one for myself. I clink her glass with my own, and tap the toaster oven—a toast to the toaster. Then I chug. I hear her yell, "So what's going on with you my darling? How was your healer?" She says the word healer like it's code for *serial killer*.

In the family room I set her glass on the coffee table, on a makeshift coaster that's really a carpet tile sample. "It was yoga," I tell her, pointing to her water.

"Oh good, I am so parched." She picks up the glass and takes a long pull. "Thank you honey. Mmm. It's delicious."

"It's tap water."

"Well, it's still *wonderful*."

I stand there, waiting for the shower to summon me.

"You're still beautiful, you know," she says.

"Whatever," I say.

She pats the seat beside her. "Come sit, my beautiful darling."

"I have a ton of stuff to do. And stop calling me beautiful."

"But honey, it's true."

"It's objectifying. And pandering. I don't need you cheerleading my looks."

"Heil Hitler!" she says, and raises a stiff arm to salute me.

"Jesus, Mom."

She looks up at me. "What? What did I say? I'm never going to forget what happened to the Jews, honey. Don't you worry." She shoves an index finger toward me then. "Because it could happen again and don't say I am acting paranoid."

"Yes, Mom. You've told me this," I say, perching on the slice of sofa she's allotted for my ass.

"You know, Eve, I've been watching you and Neil, and I know—believe me, I know—how hard marriage can be."

"You mean after three failed ones?"

"Thank you for reminding me. What I'm saying is that you two should hold hands once a day at the very least."

"What are you talking about?"

"Being a good wife."

"What the fuck, Mom? Neil and I are fine." I could tell her all about the wild sex we just had, but some things are private.

"And you really should be more supportive."

"Of who, you?"

"Sure, why not?" she says, lifting her chin.

"Because this isn't about you!" I shout.

My mother lowers her voice, showcasing her ability to talk in a controlled professional manner to a madwoman. "You know the children can hear when you disrespect me. Is that the example you want to set for them?"

"Mom, Jesus Christ, I can't say anything to you."

"I was thinking the same about you," she says, her eyes shining with implied meaning.

I sit there fuming, my shoulders heaving with decades' worth of frustration. My mother flips a page in the magazine, considers a military-themed outfit accessorized with a string of pearls.

Then the footsteps. Then the guitar. Neil's been playing the same song over and over since my mom moved in. "Wichita Lineman." He's sinking deeper into a funk, evaporating into the woodwork like a ghost.

"Mama!" Chloe runs to me and clutches my thigh.

My mother claps her hands. "Oh she is so darling," she says.

Chloe remains attached to my leg but starts jabbering away while my mother reaches out her arms listening to none of it, her hands taut, palms white.

"Grandmom, the fairy turned into a mermaid and saved the merman from the trolls and her wished a wish and her wish turned true! And Biddle is SO funny. He ate the berry and sung like a *girl*! And he has huge *eye*lashes! And Nori has blue *hair*!" She says the last word like it has two syllables—*hay-urr*.

"The what? He did? Oh you are so funny! Do you have a kiss for me?"

"I am not funny!" she shouts.

"You are *funny*," my mom says.

"I am NOT!" she screams, shrieking the last word.

"Funny girl!" my mom says.

"Mom, stop it!" I yell. "You're teasing her."

My mom purses her lips at me. "You're teaching her how to respond to me," she hisses. Then to Chloe she says, exasperated, "Come here and kiss me for God's sake."

Chloe looks up at me. "Mommy I don't want to."

"You don't have to, sweetie." I want to say, *Behold! Exhibit A!* I look at my mother with raised eyebrows.

My mother replies with a thin-lipped expression that communicates, *Now look at what you've done. You've turned her against me.* "It's okay. I didn't want a hug anyway," she says, as Chloe runs away. Then somewhere inside her a switch flips. "Is there any coffee?" she asks, coy, suddenly shy. Flirtatious even.

"It's from this morning," I say.

"That's okay. You can nuke it for me. I don't mind."

"I could make a fresh pot," I say, goading.

She perks up at this. "Oh could you?"

"You want to make it yourself? I have to take a shower."

"Not really."

"Well then, you still want the old stuff?"

"I guess," she sighs.

After preparing her mug I head upstairs wishing to God Florence Henderson was my real mother.

Afterward, I'm at the dining table folding laundry—Neil's still strumming and crooning in the basement—when Billy pulls into the driveway in his old Jeep Wagoneer. I watch him get out of the car, which suits him much better than that flashy SUV. I could watch him getting in and out of his car all day if it weren't almost time to pick up Sam from school.

"When Dad cheated on you, what did you do?" I ask my mom a few minutes later, folding a pair of miniature skinny jeans.

"Eve, where is this coming from?" she asks, laying her book on her chest. She's reading *Twilight*, and is on team Edward.

"I don't know, I was just thinking about it."

"I told you, hold hands at least once a day," she says.

"Noted, Mother."

"You're sure everything's okay between you and Neil? He seems so depressed."

"He is depressed. Just—Jesus. Just forget it."

"Well, I... Let's see," she says, biting. "What did I do. It was so long ago." I abandon my folding and resume my position on the sofa.

My mother tells me how she always suspected in the back of her mind, how friends of hers reported that they'd seen my dad with another woman at the Phila-deli, how she refused to believe them until she found the lipstick on his underwear, which might be the most disgusting image I have filed in my brain, far worse than the times I have bathed my mother. "By the time I discovered the underwear I knew the marriage was over so I just gritted my teeth and washed them."

"You didn't keep them? For evidence? I thought that was what finally—"

"No honey. Things were different then."

"How?"

She shrugs. "We were more naive. We didn't keep score. Divorce was a novelty."

"Everyone was getting one," I say.

"It was the thing to do," she agrees, nodding.

My mom tells me that it wasn't until Larry got knocked unconscious in a car accident that she finally left my dad.

"You were, what, four?" my mom says. "And Larry's friend, what was his name? The real little one with the thick glasses."

"Mike Kootchick?"

"Mike Kootchick," she says, nodding and smiling. "Mike's big sister, I'll never remember her name. Cynthia. Claudia."

"It was Cheryl."

"Something. Cheryl."

"It was Cheryl."

"Well whoever she was, she took them out for a car ride."

"It was Cheryl, Mom. Do you not believe me?"

"Oh honey, of course I do."

"So?"

"So, what was I thinking? She'd just gotten her license. What was her mother thinking? Oy."

"Yeah, really."

"Well honey, things were so different. We didn't have these ginormous car seats with all the buckles and the cup holders or any of that crap."

My mom and I crack up. "Where did you learn *ginormous*?" I ask.

"Sex and the City. Me *likey!*"

"Um, okay," I say, disturbed.

"I used to watch it every night on On Demand, when I had *cable*." She glares at me, her evil luddite spawn.

"Yeah, this ain't no five-star hotel," I say.

"I swear you're the only person I know who doesn't have a TV bolted to the wall above the mantel. What kind of American are you?"

"Mom, I have explained my reasons to you before. I'm not going into it again."

She swats a hand in my direction. "I remember everything you told me," she says. "About the brain development. And the imagination. The test scores, the stress hormones, the scientific studies. Anyway, yeah," she sighs. "We just let you roll around the car like loose potatoes."

"I used to lay on that shelf under the rear windshield."

"I remember that. While the car was moving."

"And you'd leave me in there in the parking lot while you shopped."

"If I didn't forget about you in the store." My mother cracks up like the event was adorable—worth commemorating in a scrapbook. *And this was the time when I forgot about Eve at the Penn Fruit for two hours.* The story is, one time my mom went grocery shopping and left the store without me. I was sitting in the cereal aisle shaking a box of Crunch Berries when the store manager found me, took me to his office and let me play with his price sticker gun while they tried to find my mom. When she finally came to get me two hours later she asked the manager if he wouldn't mind watching me for just one more hour so she could get her hair done, which he agreed to do, giving me the Crunch Berries, which I devoured dry, straight from the box. The manager was cute like Rick Springfield, but hairier, and he laughed when I told him knock-knock jokes. *Banana who? Banana banana!*

The explanation for the story is that my mom had a lot of nervous breakdowns. She hid in the hall closet regularly. It was like her home office. The explanation for the nervous breakdowns was her second failed marriage, to my father who used to terrorize us all with his leather belt and temper tantrums. But looking at it now, my dad had nothing on old Dick Dorian Sr. And that, at the very least, is a comfort.

"So?" I prod, but my mother remains glued to the movie

behind her eyes. I'm just about to kick her (gently) when she returns to Earth.

"It wasn't even a big crash," she says. "She got rear-ended. It wasn't her fault. And then Larry's in the hospital unconscious. I'm a nervous wreck. And your father, the jerk—*yelled* at me in the hospital for crying to the doctor, carrying on about *appearances*. With my son laying there in a coma, bruises covering half his face. He was ten years old! *That's* when I knew I was going to leave him."

I sit there shaking my head, the laundry forgotten about. "What an asshole," I say.

"What an *asshole*," she repeats. "May he rest in peace. But you said it."

My hunch is that, stroke notwithstanding, my mother views herself as the victor for outliving my father, who died of a massive coronary three years ago.

We sit there thinking about it all for a couple moments. Then I ask, "Why didn't the cheating bother you?"

"I don't know. Maybe I didn't care anymore. I was depressed. Oh Eve, it was so long ago. Why is this so important to you? Are you having an affair?"

"No! Why does everyone keep asking me that?"

My mother regards me. "I know that handsome witch doctor lives right next door. I see him laughing. He stands there and looks at that ginormous house of his and laughs! What kind of man laughs after his wife and son get killed? It's disgusting."

"Who said they were killed?"

My mom looks at me like I'm an idiot.

I exhale through my nostrils and press my mouth in a line. "Why aren't you suspicious that Neil is having an affair?" I ask.

"Oh, Eve. Get a grip, girl," she says. "After what happened last year? That man learned his lesson. I never saw a grown man cry more than your Neil. He's a goody."

"Oh yeah. He's a treasure." This is what happens when you set the bar an inch above the ground. Ninety-nine percent of all men rank "goody" status in my mother's warped eyes. If they can show remorse, they're okay in her book. But Billy laughing after his wife has died? He must be a terrorist.

"Don't worry, Mom," I say, from between clenched teeth. "Everything's fine."

"It had better be," she says, raising her chin.

Chapter 20

So, how's the writing?" my sister-in-law says, looking up from the cake she's icing, homemade pumpkin spice, smiling as if I am about to tell her all about the opus I've been working on. She's got the optimism gene and loves that I've started something creative. Maybe it's the paint fumes—she's an artist herself. And a farmer, like my brother.

"I'm just journaling for now," I say, which is partly true. I finally picked up an actual book to write in, even if I haven't picked up my pile of Post-Its, napkins and receipts from the police station. I take a large swallow of wine, scooping the sweet potatoes into a serving bowl and trying to remember not to burn the turkey. This is our first time hosting Thanksgiving, which until now was always at my mom's.

"*Journaling*," Larry says, looking up from the cranberry sauce, exploding into a fit of laughter. He can barely spit out his next insult. "When did that word become a *verb*?"

"Grow up, Larry," I say, glancing at Neil, who's stirring the gravy. I have this vision of him lunging across the room, sauce-pan in hand, to bash my brother's brains in, sending boiling gravy pouring down Larry's face.

"What do you *journal* about, Eve?" Larry says, relishing the moment. He switches to a falsetto. "Do you *journal* about your existential angst? Are you searching for meaning atop this crazy spinning blue marble? Are you finding yourself whilst *journaling*?"

"Fuck off," I say.

"Larry, would you leave your sister alone," Stacy says, shaking her head at me.

Neil peeks at the scene before him and gives me a shrug before returning to his gravy. I wonder if he secretly thinks the same thing about my 'journaling.' *Thanks for sticking up for me, asshole.*

My mother walks in clutching a section of the *Philadelphia Inquirer*, her reading glasses slipping down her nose. "Looks like they're zeroing in on a killer in that drowning," she says, glancing at me. "They found evidence of *foul play* in that autopsy. Now where did I put my wine glass?"

I grab the paper from her and scan for the article while Neil points to the table, covered with the porcelain serving dishes that used to belong to my grandmother. There among the challah stuffing, noodle kugel, whipped sweet potatoes, green bean casserole and cranberry sauce is my mother's empty glass. "Oh good," she says. "I didn't want to dirty another one."

"That guy is guilty," Larry says, walking over to me, rubbing his hands.

"Oh what, now we're friends?" I say, hoarding the paper.

"Dream on," Larry says.

"You want me to give you the bottle?" Neil says to my mom, tipsy himself. "You could drink straight from there. No glass necessary."

My mother looks at him, hand on her jutting hip. "Well if I hadn't already filled a glass I might do that," she says. "With those two for kids, I need all the lubrication I can get."

"Mom! Ew!" I scold from over the top of the paper, still searching for the article.

"You're the sick one," Larry says. "Get your mind out of the sewer." Then, "There it is." He points at a short article titled, "Forensic Evidence in Lisko-Dorian Drowning Reveals Foul Play."

Montgomery County police issued a statement Wednesday morning that the deaths of Anna Lisko and Deepak Dorian were not accidental. Deepak was just three years old when he and his mother drowned in their Wynnewood home sometime between Tuesday, October 9 and Wednesday, October 10.

The bodies of Lisko and Deepak Dorian were discovered on the morning of October 10 by Ms. Julie Parraga, 57, the family's nanny, who had previously been employed by Billy Dorian's brother Richard Dorian Jr., and by their late father, Richard Dorian Sr.

Richard Sr. served twenty years at Montgomery County Correctional Facility for the 1976 murder of his wife Justicia, which is known in local lore as "The Bryn Mawr Bludgeoning."

Forensic evidence of unlawful behavior was uncovered during the autopsies earlier in the week. "This new evidence makes it clear that the drownings were not accidental," said Lieutenant Kenneth Morgenstern Wednesday. No further information is being released at this time.

"Somebody's going to prison," Larry sing-songs. "They should cut his balls off for what he did."

"You don't know he did it," I say, wondering what was found in the autopsies, because what could have been discovered inside their bodies that wasn't apparent on the outside when they were found? Poison?

"You need to stay away from that guy," Larry says, looking me up and down. "You are a dumbass to keep seeing him."

I glare at my mom.

"What?" she says. "I love you."

"So you gossip about my life?"

"It's not gossip. It's your brother. He loves you. We all just want you to be safe. God forbid that monster takes hold of you and—oh I can't stand to think about it."

"I'm safe," I say. "See?" I slap myself in the chest. "I've spent *hours* with him—all alone in his far away office—and he is not a killer. Why doesn't anyone believe me?"

"It's not that we don't believe you," Stacy says, setting her cake on the sideboard. "It's that we don't fully trust Billy Dorian."

"And why are you so sure he's innocent?" Neil says, just as the kids come running in—Sam, Chloe and my niece Louisa, who's eleven.

"When are Aunt Jeannie and Griffin getting here?" Louisa says, clutching her belly.

"We're *so* hungry," Sam shouts, his eyebrows undulating, his feet a blur of movement on the grubby wood floor.

Chloe sucks her hair. "We can't wait anymore," she says.

"You going to share some of that with me?" I say, hooking a finger around a slimy strand and yanking it from her mouth.

"Mine!" she protests, and stuffs it back into her mouth.

I glance at Neil, who looks like he's still waiting for my answer, then walk over to the oven to check on the turkey. *Yeah, why are you so sure, Eve? Is it really because he's so good looking? Because all you can think about is schtupping him 24-7?*

"Your Aunt Jeannie is on her way," my mom says.

"Go wash your hands, guys," Neil says.

"I'll go help them," I say and herd everyone down the hall, thinking back to the summer, when I first met Anna Lisko and Billy Dorian.

"I can do it if you want," Louisa says. "I'm a mother's helper at home."

"Really?" I ask as she gets to work rolling up Chloe's dress sleeves. "Oh yeah, I do everything—diapering, feeding, putting them down for naps."

"Impressive," I say. At Louisa's age I was just starting to steal my mother's cigarettes and make out with my pillow pretending it was that blond-haired boy from *On Golden Pond*. "I'll leave you to it then."

While my precocious niece takes care of Sam and Chloe I wander into my mother's room—formerly the guest room. My mother insisted we bring the framed school photographs from her dresser. The photos are ancient, as are the frames—cloudy scratched plexiglass panels molded to stand on their own like open books. There's an eight-by-ten of Larry when he was a sophomore in high school, hellbent on growing a pair of lamb-chop sideburns. I worshipped my big brother, but all he ever did was break my toys, lock me in darkened closets and punch me in the stomach. Despite the discoloration of his teeth from whatever vitamins my mother was prescribed when she was pregnant with him, he shines.

In the photograph he wears a jacket and tie, something he never does now. This was back when picture day meant something, before peoples' lives became over-documented, when every kid but one B.O. smelling, broken-toothed hoodlum would dress to the hilt to get his portrait taken. I used to sneak up to his doorway and spy on him while he practiced his electric guitar. He used to play "Come Together" over and over. I suppose, now that I think about it, that Larry was my first crush.

Jeannie's picture is from her senior year, when all the girls wore the same black V-neck velvet top with a dainty chain around their necks. She smiles serenely, her oily nose in the air. Jeannie's girl version of Larry's face is framed with brown hair parted down the middle that she used to roll in empty orange juice cans so it would undulate in lazy waves instead of frizzing from her head like a nuclear explosion. Her forehead gleams and her collarbones jut from ballet and semi-starvation. Jeannie always liked to be in control, until everything went down with the Odious Testicle. Now she says, screw control. And screw skinniness. If she wants to eat a fucking pizza, she eats a fucking pizza.

The photo of me is from my junior year, with a smudged blue background. My dyed razored hair explodes in a spiky mushroom. I wear my black shirt buttoned to the top with a handful of crystal rosaries around my neck. The heavy black eyeliner and blood-red lipstick advertises how badly I yearned to be older then, how I longed to be anyone but me. There's no smile, not even in the eyes, but you can see the flush of youth imprisoned behind my chalky white foundation.

Once we're all seated at the table, having given up on Jeannie, I spoon turkey, mashed potatoes, and green beans on the kids' plates. We go around the table giving thanks. Chloe is thankful for mashed potatoes. Sam is thankful for his latest Bakugan, and for pumpkin pie. Larry is thankful for the bird, which has come from his farm. Louisa is thankful she's mastered a new stitch on her knitting needles. Stacy is thankful that we're all together and hopes Jeannie arrives soon. My mother echoes this sentiment and raises her glass, thankful for the wine she shouldn't be drinking.

"I am thankful for this meal, and this family," Neil says, looking at me. I know he's not being entirely truthful, that having my mother here sucks, especially now that she's doling out marital advice, but I can also tell that he's actually afraid for me, and therefore grateful for my tenuous existence.

"I am thankful for your thankful," I say to my husband of almost fifteen years.

The doorbell rings. My mother claps. "Larry go let her in," she shouts from her throne at the head of the table.

"It's not Jeannie," Larry says at the door. We all turn and see a hefty older woman standing in the doorway. I rush over to see what's going on, Neil tailing me.

"Hi," I say. "Can I help you?"

"Eve Myer?"

"Yes," I say, not feeling very good about this unexpected visitor.

"Detective Edwina Bryant in the flesh," she says, displaying her badge. Detective Bryant has a short snout of a nose, ruddy pink wattles and deflated downturned lips, which, almost as a feminine afterthought, are covered in something pearly. She wears most of her faded auburn hair slicked back, except for an over-sprayed set of baby bangs pasted to her forehead. It's such a bad look on her—on anybody—that I can't believe she's embraced it willingly. I wonder if she'd let me take a picture.

"Sorry for intruding on your family dinner," she says and I feel a curious burst of pride for how lawful we all are at this moment, even if I have been exonerated. I want to sweep my hand across the scene before me like a game show model and say, *See, Detective Bryant? See how normal we are? How innocent?* Because a part of me feels very, very guilty.

"Would you like some turkey?" I ask, but she turns it down.

"Mrs. Myer, Mr. Myer, Can I talk to you alone?" she says to me.

Neil and I look at each other. Then we usher her past the dining table, through the kitchen, into the family room, and close the door.

Detective Bryant hands me an envelope. "You never came to retrieve these, Mrs. Myer. Thought I'd save you the trip." I take the package, open it and look inside. My story ideas. Detective Bryant does not assume the typical male police stance—feet set wide, chest puffed, notebook at the ready. Instead she just stands. "I'd like to ask you a few questions about Rick Dorian," she says.

Neil and I tell her everything we know—which is not a lot—everything *except* the fact that Rick's car pulled up to Billy and Anna's house the night she and Deepak drowned. I glare at Neil as we follow the detective back to the front door. Once Detective Bryant is tucked safely inside her black and white squad car I stop

Neil from entering the house. "You lied to me," I say to him in a whisper meant to convey a yell.

"I can explain, Eve."

"I'm waiting," I say.

"I can't. Not now. Just wait. Please. It's for your own good."

"Okay, now you've got me even more suspicious. What the fuck, Neil? What happened that night?"

Neil goes down on one knee like he's going to propose. "Eve, please trust me on this one. I promise I will tell you everything once the case is resolved."

"What if he did it, Neil? Then what? Do you go to jail?"

The door cracks open and my mother is standing there. "This looks chivalrous," she says. "Can you come in or am I interrupting foreplay? Did that detective what's-her-face get you in the mood? Perverts."

"Mom would you *please*," I say, and pull the door shut. Then I shout, "We'll be in in a minute!" I regard my kneeling husband just as a second car pulls up. "Tell me, Neil," I demand, thinking that my husband looks pathetic on the ground like this.

"Eve, please," he begs and I growl in exasperation.

We both look up when we hear a car door slam and there is my sister Jeannie, trudging up the walk, unsmiling and annoyed rather than sheepish and apologetic. I open the front door for her, and Griffin follows her in, carrying a stack of bakery boxes from Carlino's, tied with red and white string.

"I brought a pumpkin cheesecake, an apple pie and a chocolate torte," Jeannie announces, leading the way, her tone devoid of holiday cheer, pointing at the sideboard where Griffin stows the desserts. She looks around the table and then at Neil and me. "You started without us?" she says at me, as I resume my seat.

"Come here my darlings and give me a kiss," my mother says from her seat. Jeannie waves her off. Griffin goes dutifully to his grandmother and allows her to sniff him and moan. "Oh God I just love you!" she shouts. And she calls *me* a pervert.

"The kids were starving," Neil says, shrugging.

"And the adults?" she asks, planting her hands on her hips. "You couldn't wait for a blood relative?" She stares us down.

"You were supposed to be here an hour ago," Larry says, regarding his twin like she's the hired help.

Griffin sits and begins heaping his plate with food. Jeannie storms into the bathroom and Larry looks at me and mouths the words, *fucking psycho.*

My mom says to anyone who will listen, "I told you, she works too hard."

"Nobody said she didn't, Mother," Larry says, stabbing a slice of turkey with his fork. "It's not like I wake up at four A.M. every single day or anything."

"Oh Larry, my sweet boy. You work hard too. You should relax more," my mother says, overcompensating, trying to elicit a conspiring gesture from Stacy.

"Are you kidding me?" Jeannie says when she returns, eyeing the wine glass in my mom's hand. She storms over, yanks it away and dumps it in the kitchen sink, shouting at us for killing our own mother. Back at the table, she grips Sam's chair back and he shrinks in his seat. "I was late, you selfish assholes," she says to us. "Not you, kids," she adds softly, stroking Sam's mop of chestnut hair, and then glares at me. "Because *your* friend was in the ER."

"*What?*" I say.

"Who?" my mother asks.

"Billy Dorian," says Jeannie. "Fucker got the shit beaten out of him."

"Language," my mother says, eyeing the bottle in the center of the table, the left side of her mouth drooping just the tiniest bit.

Chapter 21

"Hey Eve," Billy says when he comes to get me in the waiting room two weeks after his hospital stay. Instead of remaining standing, waiting for me to rise and follow him, he limps over and sits beside me on the leather sofa and smiles as if he's embarrassed by his face, which displays a rainbow of bruising, especially over his right eye. I'd been watching him feverishly from my window but all I could see was the flicker of the TV, a huddle of blankets and a bottle of pills I took to be painkillers.

"Can I get you a cup of coffee or anything? It's freezing outside."

"Sure, but—I feel like I should ask you if I can get you anything. Are you okay?" I want to reach out and smooth my thumb across his brow.

"A little tender. A little medicated. But okay."

"Oh my God, Billy. What happened? Can you talk about it?" I say, even though I already know because I read about it online. It turns out that Deepak was Rick's son, according to DNA tests. Which means that when Billy snapped at me that morning in his house when I went over with the beer and the fudge, he wasn't mad at me for hitting on him. He thought I knew the truth.

Thanks to the Internet, everyone knows that Rick has a history of violent behavior too, behavior that includes having used one of his former girlfriends as a punching bag. I've also learned that while the police investigate Billy and Rick, they are under surveillance. Not exactly house arrest, since it hasn't been proven that either of them broke the law, but it's been suggested that they both remain in the state and not plan any airplane trips for a while. Other than that, they're free to come and go as they please.

"I was in Manayunk, at a bookstore."

"Spiral Bookcase?" I say, inappropriately excited.

"Yeah you know that place?"

"It's my favorite bookstore." This tidbit of info shouldn't be important, but in a way it proves Billy's innocence. Murderers don't hang out at family-run bookstores. This place even has a cat, for crying out loud.

"I love that place," he says.

"So, what happened?"

"A couple guys in there recognized me from the news. You know, the more I think about it the more I think they were out looking for me. Following me. They jumped me in Pretzel Park. Cops let it happen. They were there and didn't break it up 'til I was on the ground for a good minute or two."

"Jesus. People are such bastards."

"That's what they think about me."

I shake my head slowly as I study his face. Even with the swelling and the bruising he is still breathtaking. Maybe more so. He's wearing one of those schmattas like a headband again, to keep the hair out of his stitches I guess.

"I'll be right back," he says, patting me on the knee. He winces as he rises. Opens a door beside his office. I can see a Formica countertop and one of those plastic countertop kettles. I pull off my hat and stuff it into my bag. Fluff my hair and tug at my sweater, wondering if he can tell I put on a little holiday weight.

"So, I have a proposition for you," he says when he returns. He sets a mug down in front of me on the coffee table.

I sit on my hands and swallow. "A proposition?" Oh Jesus. Is this going to be the part where I regret ever making an appointment?

He sits beside me, turns his body so it faces mine, props his elbow on the seat cushion. His sweater pulls tight at the armpit, tracing the slope of his bicep, which looks full and hard. He hikes his knee across the seat so that it's just grazing my thigh.

I face him, begging my body and face to act natural, remain composed. I do not move my thigh.

"Remember when you agreed to be my guinea pig?"

"For discounted healing services? I do."

"Good. So a colleague and I have been exploring the psychological aspects of chronic pain, and we want to test our hypothesis."

"And?"

"We think that by removing a patient from their comfort zone, from their normal routine, we can short-circuit the connection between the neural pathways and the site of the injury."

"Uh huh," I say, nodding as if I follow.

"We want to see if we can reboot the brain without lobotomizing the patient," he says. "See if we can manipulate the prefrontal morphology."

"Oh right. That."

"Exactly."

"And you want to try it on me?"

"You're quick," he says.

"You're going to take me out of my comfort zone?"

"Yoga."

"Yoga," I say, not getting it.

"Kids. Family. Domestic life."

I raise an eyebrow. My lips part to ask what the hell he's talking about, but no words escape.

"You've come to equate yoga and all the other stuff with pain. You said it hurts when you do yoga. It hurts you at home." He counts on his fingers. "I want you to try something completely different. Completely foreign from anything you're used to."

"What, like sky-diving?"

"Sky-diving is out of my budget. But I bet it would work."

"What is in your budget?"

"Hunting," he says.

"Hunting," I say. "Are you even allowed to—"

He frowns, looks at his hands. "The police admit that I've been nothing if not cooperative, especially given what happened with, uh..." he gestures at his battered face. "I submitted to a psychiatric evaluation and a lie detector test and I'm all clear. As long as we accept an escort, all systems are go. If you feel unsafe in any way, this will hopefully reassure you."

"What are the details?" I say.

"Deer hunting. Discussed it with my colleague, who incidentally served as a character witness for me. He gave a really wonderful testimony, has known me since, uh, forever. Anyway, voila. An experiment is born. There will be four of us. Two clients. Two healers. I'm assuming you haven't hunted."

"No." I tuck a loose strand of hair behind my ear, trying to envision spending a day in nature with Billy. Billy, whose father, a convicted murderer, loved to hunt. I'm not sure if I'm relieved or frustrated by the fact that we won't be alone. It's apparent to me that a story was already writing itself in my warped brain—that Billy was taking me to some remote mountain to have his way with me.

"Do you think you'd be okay with it?" he asks, squinting against the possibility of my rebuke.

"I read something about you and your brother," I say, stammering a little. "And your dad. I hope it's okay that I'm bringing this up."

He tilts his head, inviting me to continue. "Of course. Let's discuss whatever you want. Everything. I want you to feel comfortable with this, Eve. I know it's a lot to ask."

"Thanks. Well, I'm sure you know that there's all this stuff online about your family, about your past."

"I don't go online much," he says.

"Yeah, it's probably not a good idea," I say.

We pause to reflect. Detective Bryant would be so proud of him.

"So what's it say?" he says.

"Well, there's all this stuff about post-traumatic stress, and anger issues, and—and I can't help but think, that everything that's happening would drive even the most placid, gentle person to lose their shit. I guess I'm just—trying to ask—are you okay with not, like, exploding? Because I wouldn't be."

Billy nods. "No, yeah. I know it's—a total bitch. And I've had issues. Obviously. But what people don't see—and I understand this about our culture—the sensationalism, because it's all part of the whole—everything—is that I have devoted my life to transcending every single trigger that has caused me to lose control. I've transformed my reactivity, beliefs, attitudes... I've set my entire life up to be accountable for my actions, to cultivate integrity, to—"

"I believe you," I say. "I can't imagine how you—or anyone really—can have so much discipline—but I believe you. It's just—people are accusing you of—of—well, you know—and I don't know, maybe it doesn't even matter what I think. But from everything I've seen, getting to know you, I just don't believe what they're saying."

"Well, I think the police are with you on that. Otherwise I wouldn't be able to conduct this experiment."

"That's reassuring."

"Yeah. For you and me both," he says.

"I just—I get so angry, and then I get confused, and I have to ask you even though I know you didn't—because my mom, and Neil, and my whole family, they would never allow me to go with you. *I would not go if I didn't completely trust you.*" I start crying then and Billy looks at me with the most tender eyes—empathy for what I'm going through—despite the fact that his pain could fill an ocean, compared to my handful.

"Are you asking me if I killed Anna and Deepak?" he whispers.

"I'm so sorry," I say, nodding.

"Eve, look at me." He hooks a finger under my chin. Tilts it so that our eyes meet. He gazes at me for a few moments and then speaks. "I swear to you that I did not kill Anna and Deepak."

"I know," I say, but I still breathe a sigh of relief.

"It's all so fucked up," he says, dropping his finger, clasping his hands.

"My brother wants to cut your balls off," I say, wiping my tears and laughing at how absurd this entire situation is.

"Eve," he says softly. "I can't tell you how much it means to me."

"What?"

"Knowing that you believe in me. Really. It's been so lonely. And frustrating. And I've been sitting with it, and going to my teachers—but to have a—a friend—someone with young kids—you've just—it means a lot to me, Eve."

We look at each other and our eyes are wet. I reach out and gather him into my arms. We embrace, and I feel that engine deep inside the pit of my stomach spark to life.

He breaks away, but reluctantly. "Do you want to think about it? Get back to me?" he says, wiping his eyes without a wisp of shame.

"When did you plan to go?"

"After New Year's. If that works for you. We'd need a weekend. Friday night through Sunday."

I can feel the color rise in my face.

"A buddy of mine owns some land near Scranton. Private hunting grounds, sweet little cabin in the woods. We missed bow-hunting season, but we can get everyone for rifle hunting anywhere from now till the end of the month."

I nod, my head filling with that familiar sensation—buzzing bees or bubble wrap. A hum. A fog.

"I have an extra 30-30 you can use. Got it for my thirteenth birthday. So we'll set you up with a temporary license, do a little target shooting beforehand, have you ever fired a gun?"

"At camp," I say. "Rifle range."

"Cool," he says.

"I was a pretty good shot," I say.

The rifle range was where sluts like me went to fool around at night, the place I learned like a Pavlovian dog to equate rifles with blow-jobs. We'd walk uphill in the dark for a quarter mile. My arm would be wrapped around the boy's waist, his wrist slung over my shoulder, both of us bent on a carnal mission, hopped up on whatever sugary treat we'd sucked down at the canteen. Mildewed mattresses covered in black-and-white ticking lay in a row on a wooden platform with a shingled rooftop to keep out the rain. Fireflies bobbed around us, crickets screamed, and mosquitos bit the backs of my knees as I practiced fellatio on future litigators and gastroenterologists who marveled that one of their own would ever swallow.

Billy nods and clears his throat. "Well, how about next week, instead of coming here we meet at the gun range? I think I have a card from the place I can give you. It's south on Route One. Near Delaware. Should only take you about a half hour to get there."

"Sounds good," I say.

"So would you be my guinea pig, Eve?"

"I will," I say, feeling the strain in my face—the betrayal.

"Don't sound so enthusiastic," he says, and elbows me the way a friend or a new lover might. My heart peals and I smile sheepishly.

"That's better," he says. "I like it when you smile. Makes me think I'm doing something right."

"You're doing everything right," I assure him quietly.

Chapter 22

⤳ C ⤳

*B*illy wants to take me hunting," I say. My mouth spits out the news before our appetizers have even arrived.

"Hunting?" Neil lowers his beer glass to the table. Presses his lips together. "Is that even allowed?"

"Apparently it is."

"I don't get it."

"He's working on a hypothesis," I explain. "About removing a patient from their comfort zone, getting them away from the things in their life that trigger pain, that keep them—me—in a cycle of pain." I take a sip of my Riesling. We're sitting at Supper, which is tastefully underdone for the holiday, for the early seating prix fixe. This also happens to be the twentieth anniversary of the night we first met.

"I thought muscle spasms triggered the pain."

"I know. I thought so too. But maybe the act of hunting is so focused and visceral that it will force me to process differently than how I usually do."

"I still don't get it."

"Well it's alternative health. I guess it's supposed to be bizarre. He said it's like rebooting the brain. Something about morphology." The truth is I don't fully get it either. I take another sip of wine and savor it. The wine, I understand. It's wet and sweet and tart; you drink it and get drunk. End of story.

"And he seriously thinks this is going to heal your back?"

"He's got a hypothesis. He wants to test it. Nothing else has worked. And it was part of our deal. Half price treatment if I do this."

"You keep telling me it's feeling better."

"Well it is, but not *all* better."

He looks at the table, swallows his irritation.

"I'd like to go." It's as if the words of my sentence are shrinking as they exit the cavity of my mouth. I take another sip of understandable wine.

The waiter arrives with our appetizers. Deviled eggs for me. Salad with bacon and apples for Neil.

"So can I?"

"You don't need my permission. Do what you have to do. But promise me one thing."

"What?"

"Don't fuck him." He takes a bite of his salad. "And don't get yourself killed."

"Jesus, Neil. First of all, I am not going to fuck him. I'm married to you. Second, do you really think I'd go if I thought I were in danger? Do you really think I'm that stupid? It's not like we're going to be alone anyway. There are four of us."

"Why didn't you say that before?"

"Ugh, Neil, I don't know. Give me a fucking break for once."

"The way you give me a break?"

"I don't know what you want me to say about that. I can only forgive what I can forgive. And I'll never forget it. But—it's just— it's work. I have to *work* to look at you the way I used to." I look at my lap and realize I haven't felt in love with my husband for more than a year. I have not been excited to see him, to receive a kiss or a touch, in what feels like forever. We're stagnant and floating like that island of garbage, getting bigger and more toxic all the time.

"I know," Neil says quietly, possibly feeling the same hopelessness. Then he gives an exaggerated shrug, gesturing with his knife. "Still," he adds. "You're going to be in the woods with someone you're attracted to, someone you know is suspected of murdering his wife and kid, someone with a history of violent behavior. It does not sit well."

"Then why don't you forbid me to go?"

"Eve, you need to forbid yourself. I am not your master."

"Well, it's next weekend," I say.

"Wow. It's coming right up." He sticks a toasted walnut into his mouth as if the air around us hasn't turned thick with suspicion and guilt.

"I know. I'm sorry."

"You're not sorry, Eve."

"No, I guess I'm not," I say quietly.

"Why didn't you tell me sooner? How long have you known?" His fork hovers outside his lips.

"He told me about it a few weeks ago but he needed to square away everyone's schedule. And anyway I didn't think I needed to bring it up right away, we had no plans for anything that weekend. It's not a big deal, it's just—"

"It's just a weekend getaway with your hot murderous crush." His eyes bore into mine. The fork returns to the plate, its speared lettuce leaf quivering.

"He swears he didn't do it."

"Oh, well, in that case. By all means, please, drive out to the middle of nowhere with a potential psychopath. And hell, put some loaded guns in the car. Eve, are you fucking crazy?"

"No, just incredibly stupid, apparently," I say. "I guess it wouldn't help to add that the police believe him too."

"I hope they're right. But Eve, you know he broke a guy's jaw one time? That he set his school on fire? And that he—he punched out his college professor and got himself kicked out of school?"

"Yes, Neil. I've read it all. Every article. I've combed through the entire Internet until I reached the end of the fucking thing. And I still feel safe with him. I'd just like your blessing."

"What, like the pope? Or like the father you're always complaining you never had because he was such an asshole? You're forty-one years old, Eve, and I am not your priest, or your boss, or your father. I am your husband. I don't give blessings or orders. You are on your own with this one."

"You've been a model husband," I say, pinching the corner of my napkin.

He shakes his head at me. "You're the most stubborn person I have ever met."

"At least I'm not some depressive sap," I say. "Playing guitar all day long, singing that same stupid song over and over." I pick the fight like picking a scab. Adjust the beaded bracelet he gave me for Christmas, the one I picked out myself from the Banana Republic clearance rack.

"You're planning on fucking him, aren't you," Neil says, nodding like he's just figured out the mystery of the century. He doesn't bother keeping his voice down. He looks like he is going to stab me in the face. His hands curl into fists.

The walls lean in, the picture frames swaying from their moorings. The industrial chandelier lengthens toward our lips, stretching its wire cables to hear every syllable. The salvaged pine planks on the floor strain against their iron nails in order not to miss a single word.

"I've already fucked him," I say. "In my dreams. Every single night, and especially—especially—when I'm fucking you." The other patrons turn to look at us. A bearded man-boy in a peacoat with his aging hippie mom to my left. A young woman who looks like an art student, seated with an older man near the bar to my right. A party of four women in their fifties by the window that faces South Street. "Happy Anniversary, Neil," I say, and pop a deviled egg in my mouth.

"Happy Anniversary," he spits.

We sit there seething, in the clinking, rattling, garlicky air. I steal a glance at the bearded boy. He is working so hard not to stare. He concentrates on his bite of steak. Chews ever so slowly while staring straight at his plate, knife and fork held erect in his fleshy fists, which rest on the edge of the table. I can hear his mother swallowing her salmon. I look at their table. Even their food is cringing.

I swallow the last of my wine and a numbness takes me over then. My fingers feel like ice. My heart freezes, but there is a seed of something. Tranquility. Neil has not paid this much attention to me in ages. He's never been this angry at me before, and certainly not in public. And there's something more. It's like for the first time he sees me. The damaged me. The demon me. And he responds. And then, overcome with rage, or frustration, or I don't know—the truth—I just stand up. I stand up, nod to my husband, and slither out the door.

Chapter 23

⌣⌣⌣

ecause it is New Year's Eve, there is the requisite noise, the
metallic hats, the bawdiness. I walk through it, aimlessly at
first along South Street but the drunken college students,
clusters of homeboys and tourists preening and shouting and
standing around outside bars trying to look like they're not freezing
is too much to bear. I turn up Sixteenth Street, the noise receding
behind me. My steps fall into rhythm with my breath, which I
notice after a while is constrained. I am on automatic, practicing
Ujjayi breathing.

Tears well up, spill, trace wet lines into my freezing cheeks and
then dry in their tracks. I turn my new little shattered earth around
in my mind as if it were one of the crystal beads on my bracelet,
tiny and black with dozens of facets, each one glowing or darkening depending how the light hits. And then a light hits me. I still
don't know why Neil lied to the police about Rick. I freeze in my
tracks, look over my shoulder as if to return to the scene of the
crime, then decide against it.

I walk for miles—under the world flags along the Ben Franklin
Parkway where more revelers stumble past blowing paper horns,
past SwannFountain in Logan Square, toward the Art Museum

with its massive Greek columns, under a short tunnel and along Martin Luther King Drive where the boathouses twinkle, their illuminated outlines shimmering in the rippling mirror of the Schuylkill River. I have no idea what time it is. I haven't worn a watch since I became a mother—it always scratched the babies' heads when I nursed them. And my cell phone is dead. But I have the feeling I missed the big moment when a crowd races past me, all in running shoes and formal wear—prom dresses, tuxedos and a couple even wearing wedding dresses, hooting and hollering as they pass. One of them tosses me a red carnation and I hold it as I walk, twirling it between my fingers, then shred it to confetti and sprinkle it in my path. *He loves me. He loves me not.*

I round the bend away from the river, through Fairmount Park and head toward the once grand neighborhood of Overbrook where a few rowdy partiers shout into the night. Eventually I reach City Avenue, the four-laned thoroughfare that divides the city from the suburbs. Horns honk as cars zoom by, celebrating. My feet ache, each heel screaming with blisters. My calves throb. I can feel clear mucus collect on my upper lip as my nose goes numb. I cross the avenue to the suburban side.

More miles.

Then, finally, I arrive.

I open the door. She's asleep on the sofa in the family room, *The Age of Innocence* gently rising and falling on her chest. I lean over her, slip her reading glasses off her nose. I spread a blanket over her and head upstairs, unzipping my coat. In their beds lie my children Samuel Xavier and Chloe Eliza, unfurled stars, mouths agape and haloed with sticky white. Ice cream for dinner, I bet.

I wet a washcloth in the bathroom, take each of my children's hands, wipe them clean, caress their smooth faces. I crawl into Sam's bed and curl my body around his, the boy who changed my life by being conceived, by being born amidst my cursing and shouting and cramping and bleeding. The boy who came into the world murmuring, with open hands and a smooth brow, who stole my heart. My beautiful boy. I kiss him and cry myself to sleep in his bed.

꙳

My eyelids sting. I am filled with lightness. The sun streams through the bamboo shades. I have not seen the sunshine in so long. It lights every dust mote floating before me. I am a dust mote. I do not matter. I hover, and float away. Dead from the start, happily bobbing on a ray of sunshine, gladly disintegrating, becoming absolutely nothing. It is thrilling not to matter.

I hear my mother talking to the kids in the deafening tone she perfected teaching kindergarten in West Philadelphia for thirty years.

"Who wants Cheerios?" she hollers.

I look at the digital clock on Sam's dresser. It is eight forty-eight.

I steal out of the room and tiptoe to my bedroom.

Neil is not there.

I'm still dressed from the night before. The taffeta flower stitched to the collar of my black cardigan lies wilted and crushed. My jeans feel two inches thick, as does my face.

In the bathroom I brush my teeth. In the mirror, my eyes look abused, swollen to slits.

I shed my clothes and throw them in the hamper, crawl back into bed and shut my eyes. My mother can deal with the kids. A few hours later I open my eyes again and my husband is there. I sit up and look up at him, expectant, for what I have no idea. He leans against the dresser, folds his arms across his chest. He's wearing his coat. Is he coming or going? He clutches his gloves and hat, squeezes them so hard his knuckles match the white bedspread.

"I did a lot of thinking last night," he says and I can tell he's rehearsed his speech, the way he launches right into it, not waiting to gauge where I'm at with all this. "And I know that for whatever reason you're hell-bent on not forgiving me." There's something in his stance that tells me he no longer needs to make sure I'm okay with anything. I am no longer his responsibility, his puzzle to solve. There's something removed, a dark glint in his eyes that wasn't there before. He's no longer mine. It's a guarded, searing reminder that we are not one organism, a jolting hit of knowledge. How did I miss that obvious fact? He is his own person. And I am, for the first time in almost two decades, alone.

"I'm trying," I say, but we both know that's not necessarily true.

"I don't get it, but I guess it's not my job to understand," he says. "All I know is, I don't want to be around you right now."

I nod, and stare at his throat where his T-shirt hangs limp under his down coat.

"So, look," he sighs. "This is your chance to figure out what you want. Go on the hunting trip. Run away with Dorian if that's what you need. Just let me know when you know what you want. And make it soon. Because I cannot take much more of this."

"Okay," I say, agreeing to all of it. He's right. And it's a relief to stop pretending that we have something together.

"I'm gonna go make breakfast," he says.

"Neil," I say, my voice hoarse, the sound of a fallen beast.

He looks at me with a mixture of tolerance and disdain.

"Thank you."

His hand grips the doorknob. "I'm not doing it for you," he says, and turns to leave.

"Wait," I say.

He indulges me by standing there, fuming. "What is it."

"Why did you lie to the police?"

He sighs. "Rick saw me that night, and he came up to me and said he'd—said he'd 'make us sorry' if we didn't stay out of their business. Said he'd 'hate to see something horrible happen to Sam or Chloe.'"

I gasp as if awoken from a nightmare. My eyes fill.

"Maybe I should have told," he says, and walks out of the room as I sob, my eyes stinging with the fresh tears.

A few minutes later my mom is standing in the open doorway. Tears soak the collar of my cardigan.

"Can I come in?" she asks.

I shrug my shoulders. What does it matter. My husband hates me. I am loathsome. A real catch.

She takes two steps into the room and leans against the dresser, the white laminate falling-apart thing that used to be mine in high school, back when we abandoned our old life and moved to Chicago with her third and final husband. She crosses her arms over her chest and speaks. "Look, Eve, I know I'm no expert on relationships but I know a decent thing when I see it. It's not supposed to be perfect. It's not supposed to be easy. And that man bends over backwards to make it up to you. If you screw it up you will be sorry for the rest of your life and those kids—" She pauses, swallowing back tears. "Sam and Chloe need you two in the same house, under one roof. Period. Now," she says. I can feel her glowering at me as I stare at the old pine floor. "Stop thinking about that witch doctor this *instant* and make it up to your husband before you ruin the best thing you'll ever have."

Chapter 24

It's no more possible to stop thinking of Billy than it is to unspill a carton of milk. I don't explain this to my mother. I know what she would say: *Oh that's bullshit, Eve. You just do it is all.* But I don't just do it. I fester, and ooze, scab over, and scar. I fog up, go numb and retreat further into my mind, take deeper hits of my drug.

Neil and I steer clear of each other for the week, even though I'm dying to discuss Rick with him. But I've blown it. There's nothing we could possibly see eye to eye on right now. Not Rick, not Anna, Billy, our own kids, or what to have for dinner.

I pack the last of my things—my chipped plastic mouth guard which if I go without I will grind my teeth to powder in my sleep, my makeup bag, my journal, which I've collaged with my scribbled collection of scrap paper.

I place my bag by the door and head to the living room where Neil is tuning his guitar, and Chloe and Sam sort Pokemon cards on the rug. I kiss Sam on top of his head. "Bye Sammy," I say, but he barely looks up from his task. "Honey, can you give me a hug? I won't see you till Sunday."

"What? Oh!" he says, and hops to attention, clamping his arms around my neck for a fraction of a second. Then he's back to the cards, hunched over his spread out deck, pointing out the highest point damage cards.

Then it's Chloe's turn. "Have a good weekend, Sweetie," I say.

"Mama. Don't go," she croons. She looks into my stricken face and I dive into her liquid brown eyes, filled with innocence and possibility.

I sigh and hug her. "I love you so much," I say. "I'll see you before you know it."

Then I walk to the door. Place my hand on the knob. Look at my husband sitting there with his guitar. "Bye Neil," I say.

He turns to me. "Bye Eve," he says, his expression a study of blankness.

Billy is there in the driveway, packing his Jeep. I hoist my overnight bag higher onto my shoulder. Though this doesn't seem like an appropriate time to register what he's wearing, I do it anyway, out of a habit that began the moment we met—army fatigues, thermal shirt with the sleeves pushed up, gloves and a wool hat. He's fitting a duffel bag into the back of his car, which is covered all over in rust-colored carpet. Plumes of steam billow from his mouth.

"Hey Eve," he says, turning to me.

"Hey," I say, feeling strangled for air, biting back the tears that threaten to erupt all over again.

He turns his head slightly, peers at me curiously. "Are you okay?" He says, putting a gloved hand on my arm.

His kindness breaks me open like a geode, only instead of purple crystals inside there is only a flood of tears. He looks from side to side, as if he's about to cross a busy highway, opens his arms, and hugs me. Wrapped in his protective embrace I weep and concentrate on memorizing the feeling—his body heat, the hard musculature of his shoulders beneath the waffle-weave of his shirt, the weight of his arms around me, the sensation that there is nowhere else I'd rather be. I melt into his body while feeling my husband's eyes bore into my back from the kitchen window, but when I turn to look, no one is there. I can swear I hear the lilt of guitar strings on the freezing air.

Billy pulls away, looking concerned and possibly frightened. "Do you want to talk about it?" he says, but I can tell he'd rather not by the way he holds me at arm's length, my shoulders gripped in his hands. Anyway he's got a hunting trip to lead. And what am I going to tell him? *My husband and I are going through a rough time, and it's all because I'm crazy about you.* I wipe my tears away, admire the wood veneer on the sides of the car, the chrome door handles, the perfectly flat windows.

"You sure you're okay?" he says, studying me.

I nod more vigorously than necessary.

He rubs the scar above his eye. "Well, why don't you put your bag back here and hop in. We'll get going in a minute."

"Okay." I offer him my bag.

"I hope you packed warm clothing," he says.

"Twelve layers," I say, forcing a smile.

A police car idles at the curb, waiting.

We drive through the January evening up the winding River Drive, following the curving road where great gaping boulders and tree roots protrude, snow piled upon their unruly surfaces. The tail-lights on the car ahead of us blur and smear through my tears.

"Anna never allowed guns in the house," he explains when we arrive at his office. "I'll only be a couple minutes. Do you have to use the bathroom or anything?"

I shake my head and watch him go, wondering if it's a good sign that he follows his dead wife's rules. When he returns he's got two long black canvas cases.

❧

After an hour of benign conversation we travel in silence, exhausted by the rigor of acting normal. Eventually I fall asleep and dream of turquoise water, white sand and palm trees. When I open my eyes, Billy is on the phone. "Joint stiffness, huh," he says, his brow creased with frustration. "All right. Warmer temps. Got it."

I watch as he presses END and turns to me. "Looks like it's just going to be you and me," he says.

I swallow. Hard. "Oh," I manage.

"Yeah. They bailed," he explains. "There was a temperature issue with the client. Her joints act up in the cold. They'll try in the spring."

I frown and turn to face the window. "And here I thought this was all a ruse."

Billy peers at me, a curious smile teasing the corner of his mouth. "I don't even know what to say to you right now."

"No need to say anything," I say, wishing I'd never opened my mouth. "It's just—I have a ginormous imagination," I admit.

"I'll bet you do," he says, smiling to himself, very much not clarifying what the hell I've just blurted, thank God.

"What?" I say, belting him on the arm with the back of my gloved hand.

"I just bet you do," he says, explaining nothing.

I tear my eyes away from his profile. Then, "Is it weird that my mother loves that word? *Ginormous*?"

"Your mother," he says, shaking his head. He lets out a whistle.

"Yeah," I agree, sighing. "She's a handful."

Soon we're pulling into a narrow driveway beside a tiny cabin in the woods, snow all around. The police car pulls in behind us, makes a U-turn, and drives away.

"He'll be back tomorrow before sunrise," Billy says when I watch the squad car disappear. "Don't worry, okay?"

I nod, and we head inside.

The main room contains an open kitchen, a dining table and a couple of rattan sofas. It's large enough to fit eight twin beds along the opposite wall, each with its own night table and lamp. It reminds me of an old fashioned hospital or a camp bunk. There's a fireplace in the center of the room, with an opening on either side and a black chain curtain. A rainbow of unromantic beanbag chairs dot the circumference, slouching on the bare pinewood floor. Who the hell is going to sit in those? I wonder, rubbing my back.

Billy motions for me and I follow him up the stairs.

A queen-sized bed takes up nearly all the floor space. This must be the master suite. The room is more like a crawl space, with sloping walls that meet at the highest point above the bed, with its handmade quilt and faded ochre-patterned sheets from the seventies. "Sorry it's such a tight squeeze," Billy says, watching me bow my head as I dump my bag on the bed. "Kind of a sick joke when you have back pain, huh?"

I nod. Force a smile. Wonder where he'll be sleeping.

"Bathroom's through that door," he says, pointing. "Be a good idea to go straight to bed. Four a.m. wake-up call."

"Thanks," I say and Billy offers a charitable smile. He seems nervous. Off his usual smooth game.

"All right. You need anything before I turn in?"

"No, I'm fine."

"Good night, Eve."

"Good night," I say, certain he can read my confusion and desire like tea leaves.

Lying in bed I wonder if Billy is thinking of me—or worse—if he can read my thoughts like Anna could. He's just one flight of stairs below. Even as we share the same roof I realize I miss him, miss my appointments in his darkened office, his undivided attention, his fingers decoding my pain, untangling me. I fall asleep trying not to imagine him sneaking in here and cradling me in his arms.

❦

Billy cracks the door open and calls, "Time to wake up." Even groggy with sleep I open my eyes to search his silhouette for signs of affection, making sure to tighten my lips closed around my bite guard. I lurch out of bed and hobble into the bathroom. It's a good thing I've packed my belongings in order, with my underwear on top and my heaviest layers on the bottom. I dress swiftly, tucking every shirt into its coordinating bottom—tank-top into underpants into knee socks, lightweight polypropelene into silk long underwear into SmartWool socks, expedition weight into expedition weight into thick wool socks, fleece into fleece, and so forth until I look like a marshmallow. In the mirror I barely recognize me. I don't know where I am, where I start or end, where I'm headed or where I'll wind up. And despite my cocoon of protection, I feel more lost and vulnerable than ever.

Chapter 25

꠵꠵

"The most important thing is to stay quiet and patient and still," Billy says from the driver's seat, which sends me into another peal of giggles like a scolded child. The surreal quality of this weekend combined with this new sensation of being unmoored from my identity has caused a massive fissure in my ability to behave in any acceptable manner. Laughter has entered my veins like carbonated bacteria, and the more Billy speaks, the more I itch with my fizzy new disease.

"I'm sorry," I weep. "I'm just really tired."

"Well I'm glad to see you're in a better mood," he says, which makes me laugh harder.

The Wagoneer's headlights illuminate white flakes swirling ahead of us in the blackness. We are the only car on the highway.

I rummage through my backpack one more time in my stupor, patting down my snacks—dried apricots, dark chocolate, organic beef jerky and a bottle of water. I have no idea what to expect so I've brought a bit of everything—Band-Aids, lip-balm, camera, cell phone, hand warmers in little plastic packets. "Hungry?" I say, holding up the chocolate bar.

"Maybe later," he says, in full-on business mode.

"I don't get it," I say. "We sit like statues, but we're wearing Day-Glo *orange*. How do the deer not see that?"

"They can only see the movement, not the color. Convenient, huh?" Billy says, finally showing a scrap of his usual pith.

"I don't buy it," I say, crossing my arms and looking out the window.

"She's a live wire," Billy says to his imaginary friend.

"It's the exhaustion," I explain, flopping my head against the seat back. And the nerves. *I shouldn't be here,* I keep thinking. *I'm already cheating. This is wrong. I should make him turn around right now and take me home.*

"Did you get a good night's sleep?" he says, glancing at me and looking genuinely interested in what I have to say about it. I nearly sigh from his attentiveness.

"Yeah. Great," I lie. "I'm just not used to waking up at four. And I'm concerned about the snow."

"Ah," he says, and nods. "The snow's good. Know why?"

"Why?"

"Makes it easier to drag the carcass out," he says.

"Good to know," I say, giggling again, still not asking him to turn the car around.

"And it's good for tracking too."

I nod. "Of course it is."

When I glance over Billy is staring at me.

He stops the car at a red light. This is it. My chance to tell him I can't go through with it. But when I open my mouth, nothing resembling a protest comes out of my mouth. Instead I just say, "It's just bizarre," I say. "This whole thing."

By the time we get out of the car, one little corner of the sky has begun to brighten, like a page about to be turned. Billy reminds me to be quiet and I finally obey, maybe because I am really here now, being bitch-slapped by the freezing cold and handed a rifle.

We walk, just the two of us on a narrow path lined with scrubby trees and burrs that catch on the canvas of my borrowed coat.

Billy has outfitted me, over my many layers, in head-to toe orange, including a fleece face mask, which makes me feel about as sexy as a fire hydrant. Meanwhile my healer is decked out in sensible army camouflage and combat boots with a simple orange vest, looking as if he could film an action sequence in a blockbuster at any moment. It's like I'm walking on the moon, insulated against the elements, puffy and thick and half-deaf from my swaddling. Every step I take is slow and measured. The only sound I hear is my own breath.

He nudges me on the elbow. I have to turn my entire torso to look to where he is pointing. There's a narrow tree trunk, only a couple inches in diameter, with a chunk of its brown bark abraded so that the white inside glows, vulnerable and raw.

"It's a deer rub," Billy explains. "The bucks come and scrape it with their antlers. It's a signal. For a mate."

Only my eyes and the bridge of my nose are visible when I look at him and nod my understanding. His face is similarly covered in black fleece. A little way down the path he nudges me again. This time I look up and see a black metal bench lashed to a tree. It looks like a ski lift, a spindly perch in the sky with a shallow slatted floor attached. Billy takes my backpack and my rifle and I climb up. I sit on the left. He places our things by my feet, climbs up and sits to my right. There is no one else around. I stare into the frozen forest wondering, what is the protocol for the lovesick patient of her healer on a therapeutic deer-hunting trip?

The sky lightens a little more, a curtain rising.

Ahead of us juts a bluestone ledge covered in snow. About six feet below the ledge the forest continues, beech, ash and oak trees imprinted on the sky, black against steel, their branches outstretched hands reaching for heaven. Nothing moves around us except the steam that escapes through our face masks.

We sit in silence for an hour. Maybe two. Maybe twenty minutes. Enough time for me to experience how cold it is out here. I do not say a word because I am trying to be a good hunter. A good patient. A good little girl. I am afraid if I say anything at all it will be a complaint about the cold.

Finally I break the silence. I whisper, "Have you had any other—I don't know—telepathic—experiences since, you know—"

"Since the workshop?" he says.

I nod.

He shakes his head. "It was so weird," he says.

"I'm so embarrassed," I say into my gloves.

"Why?"

"I kissed you."

"I kissed you," he says, echoing me. "It was reciprocal."

"This is not happening," I say, my heart pounding scattershot through my body. I am so thankful to be wrapped in layers of fleece right now.

"It got me thinking," Billy says. "Do you think there's any way that Anna really could—nah. It's absurd, right?"

"What, read peoples' auras?"

"Yeah, but not just that. Do you think she could, I don't know."

"Billy, do you really not know?"

"Know what, Eve?"

"She was telepathic. She planted images into my head. And she could read my thoughts."

"God dammit," he says, and buries his face in his hands.

I have to turn my entire body to see him.

"I just don't know why she kept me in the dark," he says. "And why she told you everything."

"She told me very little. She showed me a lot, though."

Billy shakes his head.

"I think she was trying to protect you," I say.

"From what? From who?"

"I don't know."

"Eve, you have to tell me everything she said—or showed you before she—"

I tell Billy about the images. I tell him that her powers only worked within the walls of a house, like a cordless phone. I tell him about the crystals.

"Was there anything else?"

"She wrote about me in her diary. She liked me. The police told me that it was part of the evidence that exonerated me."

"She thought you were great. Told me how refreshing it was to meet someone who was literally incapable of bullshitting."

"I don't know if it's a blessing or a curse," I say in a morose monotone.

"It's a blessing, Eve," he reassures me.

I stare into the woods, my heart thundering into action yet again. I cannot stop my body from responding to this man. Maybe if I stare straight ahead for the rest of the day I can erase the allure of him. Scrub it from my skin. I hate it, how attracted I am to him, how badly I want to wrap my naked body around his. It horrifies me.

Then I remember something else. "She gave me a dolphin sounds CD. I didn't bring that. I was actually going to toss it. I hate those things."

"They're pretty bad," he jokes.

"I still don't understand how you—or she—saw into peoples' minds," I say.

"Anna had a gift. And someone she knew must have been threatened by it."

"Is Deepak—did he know you weren't—"

"Yes and no." He sighs. "He's so young. We didn't tell him. We were going to wait until he was a little older. So he could process it. But he's always been afraid of Rick."

"I noticed."

"That night at the housewarming?"

"He was running away from him," I say.

"He's done that before. It drives Rick insane."

"Insane enough to hurt him?"

Billy exhales a great white plume of steam. "It's a long, complicated story."

"Do you want to talk about it?" I say.

"Sure. What else we got going on? The deer can wait, right?"

"I think so," I say, looking around the metallic forest.

"Anna was with someone else before me," Billy says.

"Rick?"

"It's pretty unorthodox, huh."

"You don't hear about that kind of thing a lot."

"No, you don't."

"At first they were a good couple. But she got pregnant right away, and Rick started—" Billy exhales. "He started losing his temper. Drinking. A lot. He didn't want to lose her or Deepak. So he um, asked if I'd take care of them. I would be a sort of security guard. Rick can't get very far with his bullshit around me."

"So she would live with you and you guys would raise Deepak."

"And Rick would stay in their lives, from a safe distance."

"Jesus."

"Yeah. And then he met Beth, and the two of them have been inseparable. Anna tolerates her but I think she's the best thing that ever happened to him."

"She seems really—"

"Bland? Accommodating?"

"Uh, yeah," I say.

"She's perfect for him."

"His own personal Soon-Yi," I say.

"Exactly."

"Does she know?"

"Beth is the kind of person who chooses what she sees. She stays out of it, doesn't ask questions. She had a rough time growing up, and I think she just wants the security."

I sit there taking it all in, watching the steam billow from our mouths. "That is the weirdest thing I've ever heard," I say finally. "I mean I thought my family was fucked up."

"Yeah we're pretty screwed up, huh."

"But I've seen Rick and Anna. Together."

"Rick takes what he pleases. Anna can't say no to him. Beth wears blinders."

"I see," I say, knowing all too well what it's like to be so attracted to someone you can't refuse. "So what about you? Did you want to be a part of this plan?"

"Not at first. But I loved Deepak. And I had just broken up with someone I'd been with for a few years, decided I wanted to be unattached for a while... But more than that, I just figured it might be a good way to make sure that Deepak was safe and secure. Lot of good it did in the end," he says, his voice suddenly hollow.

"The pet project?" I ask.

"Yeah. I think Rick felt pretty guilty. Not that he'd ever admit it. But he wanted to do the right thing. He uh, he hurt Deepak a few times. And he couldn't live with himself."

"That boy was something else," I say.

"Yeah," he says softly.

We sit in remembrance for a few moments.

"Do you think he had anything to do with—"

"I don't want to think that. I know he did hurt her, though. Broke her arm once, trying to keep her from running out of the house with Deepak, when Deepak was one."

"Jesus. But. I still don't get it. What if you met someone that you, you know, wanted to be with?"

"Anna and I had an agreement. It also didn't hurt that neither of us were looking."

"Did you guys ever…"

"No. She was a sister to me. She loved Rick. She was heartbroken over how it turned out."

"So, who else could it be? What about Beth? You said Anna didn't really like her."

"Anna hated Beth. Beth steered clear of Anna. I don't know. I've thought it too but for some reason, it just doesn't seem likely. Beth has a good thing with Rick and she tolerates so much. Why would she risk it all?"

"Julie's no picnic either," I say. "She's so serious, and she seemed to have Deepak wrapped around her finger. It was like Anna wasn't even a blood relation when she was around. The way Deepak clung to her the night of your housewarming. How he spoke Spanish. Anna just looked so helpless and sad."

"Julie's been with our family for years. She's been incredibly loyal."

"Yeah, but she still seemed so weird with Anna."

"She's stiff, I admit. And she has always favored the men in the family."

"Where is she now?"

"Peru. With her daughter."

"What were you and Anna fighting about the night she died?"

Billy leans against me the slightest bit, enough to electrify the entire right side of my body deep within my orange cocoon.

"This is the part I can't forgive myself for. She wanted me to leave. She was planning to see Rick. She packed a bag for me. I thought she was out of her mind and I wasn't going to go, but then I just got so mad I flew out of there in a rage and it was the last time I ever spoke to her. Deepak was crying. It was horrible. It will forever be the worst moment of my life."

"You must have been terrified."

"I was. She couldn't control it. Her attachment to him," he says, his shoulders slumping.

"Did she tell you take Deepak? Or Julie?"

"Deepak had been sleeping with Julie in her room. How's that for bizarre? But Anna wanted to validate his affection for her, as much as it hurt."

"Wow," I say. "I don't think I'd ever be able to…"

"Anna liked to give."

"You think it's partly what, you know—" I can't bring myself to finish the sentence.

"Killed her? I think about that all the time."

Chapter 26

he day keeps presenting itself to us, unfurling. I forgo eating a snack or taking a picture because the only way to endure the cold is to sit perfectly still with my spine ramrod straight and I am afraid the slightest movement will send me into a spasm of shivering. My boots were guaranteed on the little tag chained to the lace hole to keep my feet warm in negative forty degree weather. They have failed me. And my sock layers are too thick to jam a hand warmer packet inside.

Billy tells me to wiggle my toes, to keep doing it, no matter how badly it hurts, and gets a couple hand warmers for me to squeeze inside my gloves. My toes ache, and it doesn't help that we see nothing, no deer, no rabbits, not even a black-capped chickadee.

I place all of my concentration into my seated posture. I take long, measured Ujjayi breaths and count the number of Xs I can spy in the tree branches. When I reach fifty I lose interest and wonder where the deer are. We've heard two shots since we got here, both from far off, and both times Billy has said that he hoped the shots would bring some action our way. He props our rifles onto two flimsy looking Y-shaped sticks in front of us, just in case.

But nothing comes.

And we sit perfectly still, saying nothing. Waiting.

And nothing comes.

And nothing comes.

And nothing comes.

And then it does.

Below our balcony platform, the stage suddenly comes to life as a huge buck enters from the right. Billy digs a knuckle into my thigh and I interpret it to mean that I am to shoot this majestic creature.

All at once, with the appearance of the buck, I forget about my frozen toes. Warmth and stillness possess me. The only sound I hear is the rush of blood in my head. Breathing ceases. I curl my exposed finger around the trigger, keeping the target in my cross-hairs, and squeeze.

My body barely registers the recoil, just like he'd described, because of the adrenaline. The bullet screams. My ears throb.

I must have shut my eyes because when I open them I see only forest—bare and metallic, the thin layer of snow blanketing the fallen leaves and the bluestone ledge below us. Behind the lattice of tree branches the sky shrugs, smudged and dull. The bullet's echo ricochets through the woods. Smoke from the rifle singes my nostrils on its way to the sky.

It must have darted away. It must have seen me aiming at it. But Billy leans his padded body into mine and I feel its solid pressure, its weight. "You nailed it, Eve," he whispers. His face is close enough to mine that the warmth of his breath caresses my exposed eyelids and the bridge of my nose.

My eyebrows raise with disbelief as I put the safety on and peer at him.

He pulls his mask down and points down at the ledge. I stand up to get a better look. There, just under the slab of snow-covered stone lay the buck, shot just below the shoulder as I was instructed.

The bright red wound, no bigger than an open mouth, greets me, garish and glistening, lipstick on a corpse.

I gasp, pulling the fleece mask away from my nose and mouth, aware suddenly of how much moisture has collected from every breath I've taken since five o'clock this morning. The mask is soaking.

"You're a natural," Billy says. His smile is wide, eyes bright. His nose is running.

I press my padded body to his, reach my arms around him, bury my face into his sliver of unprotected neck and inhale his woodsmoke scent.

Tears springing to my eyes, I whisper into his fleece covered ear, "I love you." The words escape from my mouth of their own volition, freed after being held in check for so long within the walls of his examining room. I watch as they burst through the confines of my life like slow-motion bullets, decimating miniature floating cutouts of my husband, my son and my daughter.

I.

Love.

You.

The three words hang in the sky like dying fireworks, glittering in mid-air, reliant on nothing but our shared breath.

We remain embracing, three, four, five beats. Then he pulls away, taking my Gore-Tex covered hands in his and says, "Eve." He exhales a cloud of steam that scrambles my *I love you* into a meaningless jumble. Looks into my eyes with more tenderness than I deserve. I deserve to die.

"Eve…" he starts. "This isn't why I…" he starts again but trails off. Opens his mouth as if he's going to say something more, and then says, "Fuck it."

He kisses me.

I didn't mean to pull the trigger. I didn't mean to shoot. It just came out, I swear. *So much blood.* I feel like screaming, shooting myself, vanishing into his lips. When we pull away we stare into each other's eyes, to make sure the other is all right. To make sure this is real. This moment I've fantasized about—that he knows I've dreamed of—for months.

We're still breathing and alive. Steam tendrils from our mouths. We kiss again, our lips warming each other's, sending life, desire, relief pulsing between us. I could kiss him forever. *You are so beautiful,* I think and he pulls me closer.

When we finally stop, I look back at the deer lying on the frozen ground. My stomach begins to churn as my toes return to their formerly agonized state. The sky dims. I have really done it this time. I couldn't keep my thoughts inside. Even if I wanted to.

So much blood.

Billy pulls a gleaming, menacing hunting knife from the sheath in his belt and hands it to me. Without meeting his eyes I take the knife and turn it in my hand until the sun's reflection on the blade blinds me.

Chapter 27

've sliced its throat to bleed it after Billy set it on an incline,
working as if I have not just told my healer that I am in love with
him, as if we did not just swirl our tongues around in each other's
mouths. He takes over the field dressing in the same mute manner
when the blood flow slows to a trickle, and I stand back to watch.
He eviscerates the buck, working with an efficiency that awes me.

Billy removes the entrails all the way to the deer's anus. I hold
the rear legs apart so he can work easier. We lean over the corpse,
fascinated as little boys. The intestines glisten and steam escapes in
thick clouds. I inhale the hot mushroomy odor.

We take turns dragging the buck out of the forest so that I can
rediscover what my body is capable of, what bodies have been
doing since the dawn of man, after being told so many times to
restrict my various movements. The squad car is waiting by Billy's
jeep, ready to escort us.

On the way back, we leave the deer at a friend of Billy's who
butchers game in his automotive shop. In the cabin, we're too tired
to do anything more than sip instant soup from tin mugs and stare
at the fire he's made.

That night, lying in bed, I weep, burying my face into my

pillow. The door squeaks open and a hand strokes my hair. "It's okay," he says over and over.

"It's not okay," I wail, burrowing deeper into the musty pillow.

"You're so hard on yourself," he says. "I can barely sleep."

"I feel so guilty."

"I can tell."

"I'm married. To a decent guy. And I've been a shit to him. He doesn't deserve this."

"No. He doesn't. But neither do you, Eve."

I don't say anything. I'm paralyzed with agony.

"If you want I'll go." He gets up, moves toward the door.

"Wait. Billy." I sit up, look at him standing there, wearing nothing but a pair of white pajama bottoms.

He sits on the bed. I pull him toward me, pull him on top of me. His arms frame my face as he braces himself above me. Plank position.

"You sure you want to do this?" he says and I pull myself up to his mouth, answer him with a kiss. He answers me back. Chaturanga.

The weight of his body presses against mine. The feel of his skin, of his hard muscled back, shoulders, chest. The scent of him. The taste. His lips on mine, on every inch of my body. The hot, hard erection pressed against my thigh. His hands cradling my face, squeezing my breasts and ass. His cock when it slips inside. His ass. I can't spread my legs wide enough to swallow him whole, like a snake. The mounting pleasure, the pain of it, the throbbing. Tongues darting. Eyes locked. Throats gleaming. My tongue tracing the rim of his perfect ear. The nape of his neck with my hand wrapped around it. Pressing. Pushing my hips into his. Bellies slapping. Sliding. "Oh God," we say in unison, cresting, gazing into each other's eyes. "Oh my fucking God." *Oh. My. Fucking. God.*

✦

"Good morning," he says and I open my eyes to this bright new reality. He's propped on an elbow, staring at me.

"Morning," I say.

"How's your back?"

I arch my back and then tuck my tailbone, chasing the usual sensation. "You know, this is going to sound crazy, but I swear it doesn't hurt nearly as much as it has these past few months."

He kisses me lightly on the lips and steals out the door.

I stretch like a cat in the sun then curl into a ball. As I brush my teeth a giddy feeling settles over me. My face in the mirror looks more relaxed and serene than it has since the kids were born. I dress warmly in leggings and a long cardigan, run my fingers through my hair. I ask myself if I'm ready to leave it all behind for this man. Shuttling the kids back and forth. Child support. Lawyers. Maybe we can call a truce. Figure out some civilized way to part, Neil and I.

In the kitchen, Billy's got a couple skillets going. Two steaming mugs of coffee sit on an old distressed wooden dining table. I pull my sweater sleeves over my hands and cradle my cup, taking careful sips and peering at Billy over the rim. I watch as he piles our plates with pancakes and sausage he found in the freezer. We devour in silence. Every now and then he looks at me and smiles.

After, I take our plates to the sink and wash them. Refill our mugs. He walks up behind me and I can feel his erection through his jeans. My belly begins to tingle as he slips a hand around my front and down my pants, circling around my clit, pressed up against me the whole time. Behind me he unzips his jeans and pulls my pants down to my knees. He grabs me by the hair and forces me over to the table. I splay my hands out as he pushes my head all the way to the table's surface. I scratch at the wood as he takes his cock and slips it inside me. "Oh," he moans, because I am already so wet for him. With one hand still gripped to my hair, the other continues to prod me, sweeping around, flicking expertly just like I'd imagined. I begin to moan and he joins me, the two of us throbbing and wet and full. I shout, "Fuck!" and explode. Then lie there, spent and trembling, the aftershocks of my orgasm sending jolts through my breathless body.

When we're all packed and ready to leave Billy steps into my room. As he fingers a lock of my hair I say, "Do you think Anna wanted this?" and he answers me with a kiss so tender it's like a breeze. A kiss that grows deeper. A kiss that leads to one final mind-blowing fuck, because we cannot keep our hands off each other.

When we're lying there after, staring at the ceiling, I see something glimmering—a sticker someone's left, one of those silvery prism things my kids love. I stand on the bed, reach for it and peel it off.

"What is it?" Billy asks.

"It's a fish," I say. "A dolphin." For the first time, I look around the room, at the wallpaper. It's that photographic stuff from the seventies. A beach. Palm trees. Dolphins.

Dolphins.

Oh my God.

"What is it?" he asks.

"We have to get back right now," I say, and yank on my underwear.

The whole way back my mind unravels. It counts the times Anna has tried to communicate with me. "Crazy," I say. It's the only word that seems able to emerge from my mouth. "Crazy." I say it over and over. Billy takes my hand and holds it tightly in his. We drive through the steely day, leaving the forest and the buck far behind us.

Chapter 28

My mother is throning it up on the sofa in the family room with an issue of *Us Weekly*, a subscription she insisted I buy with a Groupon she graciously presented to me, since we have no cable. "Neil and the kids went for bagels," she says, barely looking at me, which is just as well because despite her general cluelessness and her freshly compromised brain cells, the woman knows me. If she happened to study my face or the slope of my posture I swear she'd know.

Luckily I don't have time to ruminate over that, or lose it over the fact that one weekend without me has resulted in the shithole I see before me. My family's crap is lying everywhere. Guitar picks, pill bottles, magic markers, half-finished drawings, crusty milk glasses, newspapers, Legos, Neil's giant book of the *The New York Times* crossword puzzles spread open on the coffee table.

I text Billy and ask him to come over and help me search.

"How was your highly unorthodox hunting trip with *the accused*?" my mother asks, her face still buried in the tabloid.

"It was great," I say, ignoring her passive-aggressive bait. "I got a big one."

"You shot Bambi?" my mother says, folding the magazine

over so she can finally look at me. "Such a barbaric goyishe pas-time. I swear, Eve, sometimes I feel like I don't know who you are anymore."

"Yeah well, neither do I," I say.

Billy arrives and my mother glares at him, and then me. She squints, studying me.

"Mom, I don't have time to explain but Billy is innocent. Do you think the police would let him take me hunting in the middle of nowhere if he wasn't? Seriously?"

"The police these days have their heads up their big fat rear ends," my mother reasons, still staring.

She begins shaking her head slowly when I say, "I need to look for something in the sofa. You have to get up. Now."

We're turning over the living room when Neil and the kids arrive. "What's going on?" Neil says. "What's *he* doing here?" He thrusts a hostile finger at Billy.

"That's exactly what I was thinking," my mom says, resettling herself on the sofa after I've finished tossing the cushions.

Billy walks over to Neil and holds out his hand. "Get out of my house," Neil says, ignoring Billy's conciliatory gesture, nearly spitting with fury. Billy looks at me, mouths the word *sorry* and heads for the door.

"No!" I shout.

"Mommy!" Chloe and Sam say, and run into my arms, swiveling their little heads at the same time to look at Billy. "Daddy bought me a pumpernickel swirl!" Chloe says.

"That's great, honey," I say.

"Is that the witch doctor?" she says.

Sam's interest is piqued. "You mean *wizard* doctor?" he says, referencing Harry Potter.

"Are you a real witch doctor?" Chloe says, looking at Billy. "Grandmom says you are."

"That's supposed to be between you and me, dearheart," pipes my mom from the sofa, her shiny face reddening.

Billy looks from Sam to Chloe. "Some people think so," he says. "It depends on what you believe. You guys believe in magic?"

Chloe jumps up and down. "Yes!" she says.

"Not really," Sam says. "I have a magic kit, so I know how all the tricks work."

"So then," Billy says. He looks at Chloe and says, "Yes." He looks at Sam and says, "And no."

To Neil I say, "He stays. He's helping me look for something very important." To everyone I ask, "Has anyone seen that dolphin CD Anna gave me?"

"The what?" Neil says.

"Can I use your laptop, Mom?" asks Sam, already onto the next thing, reaching for my computer on the side table.

"You don't want to help find something very important?" I say, looking down at him.

"Not really," he says. "So can I?"

"Yeah, fine," I say.

"Awesome!" he says, gives me a thank you squeeze and runs up to his room with my computer, the charger cord trailing behind him.

"That cheesy dolphin sound CD," I say to Neil. "Anna gave it to me. Do you remember where I put it?"

"Eve, are you kidding me?" Neil says, still glaring at Billy, who's rummaging through a stack of Lego Ninjago paperbacks. "You think I'm about to help you with *anything* right now?"

"Forget it," I say. Then, "Billy, why don't you look in the basement."

Billy looks to Neil for directions. Neil turns away from him, storms into the kitchen with his paper cup of coffee and a brown bag.

"It's through the kitchen," I say, and run upstairs to my bedroom, nearly upending the mattress looking for the damn thing. It's not in the night table drawers, or the desk, or in the bathroom, or in the stacks of books on the floor. It's not on any windowsill. It's not in Chloe's room, where she's sitting on her floor, which is curiously littered with flakes of uncooked oats, hacking the hair off her American Girl doll with a pair of Fiskars. It's not in Sam's room where he sits on his unmade bed with his shoes on, one finger half-way up his nose, the other filthy paw on my white laptop. I don't even have time to shudder.

When I get downstairs Neil has Billy by the throat on the sofa. My mother stands near the fireplace, shouting encouragement at my husband. "Kick his ass!" she shouts, pumping her wrinkled fist in the air.

"What are you doing?" I shout. "Are you insane?"

"I'm gonna kill him!" Neil shouts.

"Let him go you stupid asshole!" I say, trying to tear his hands away from Billy's throat.

"I can smell you on him. I know you guys got together, you fucking whore-slut!"

"My daughter the slut!" my mother wails. "Just like she was in high school!"

"Mom you're such a bitch!" I shout. Then, "Neil, stop! He's turning purple!"

"I'm not stopping until the fucker's dead!" he says.

"Atta boy," encourages my mom.

"What, so you can be a murderer too? Are you retarded? Get off him!" I shout.

Neil lets go, panting, red-faced, his jacket all cockeyed and his hair, what's left of it, standing on end, electrocution style. Billy sits up on the sofa gasping for air. I rush over to him, put my arms around him. "Are you okay?" I say, running my hands through his hair. "Stop, Eve," he chokes, pointing at Neil.

"Oy vey," my mom says. "I need a nap." And with that, she lumbers out of the room.

"Yeah, stop, Eve," Neil says. "Please."

"Oh fuck you," I say, and storm out, on my way to the minivan. I search all those weird little compartments and am just about
to slam the door when I see the corner of something sticking out
from under the seat. I yank it out. The case is cracked. *Pleaseplease-
please.* I pry it open. It's there. It's whole. I rush inside.

"Sam!" I shout, running up the stairs to his room. "Mommy
needs the laptop."

"After I finish this level," he whines.

"Sam, this is an emergency. I need the laptop now."

"But Mom, you just gave it to me," he protests.

"And now I'm taking it back. Hand it over."

"No," he says, resentful of this affront on his precious computer
time. Just then Neil swoops into the room like a psychotic super-
hero and yanks the computer from Sam's grasp.

"Daddy, no!" he wails.

"Later, Sam," Neil says and hands me the laptop.

"Thank you," I mutter.

Neil growls at me. Literally growls at me.

I back away, turn and run down to the living room, Sam howl-
ing behind me.

Billy's turned back to an acceptable shade of pink. I'm about to
open my mouth to ask if he's okay but he puts his finger to his lips
and gestures at Neil, who is still growling, this time at Billy.

I slip the CD into the computer. I expect iTunes to open right
up and start downloading but the DVD player opens instead and
soon I'm looking at Anna Lisko, who is so breathtaking I realize
I'd forgotten how beautiful she was. She's sitting in her bedroom
but it's not overflowing with fabric the way it was during the house
tour. The walls are bare plaster. I can tell it's the bedroom though
because she's on the bed and it's got that ornate headboard. She's
wearing a pale blue camisole with nothing underneath and no
makeup. There are dark circles under her eyes.

"If you're watching this, it means I'm dead," she says flatly.

We all turn toward the computer and gasp in unison.

I bring the laptop over to the sofa and sit with it on my lap. Neil and Billy flank me on either side. We stare into the glow.

"Nobody listens to these dolphin things. It would take a lot to get someone to play this CD. So that's how I know. I want to thank you, whoever you are, for putting two and two together, for heeding the signs, and believing in me."

Billy claps a hand over his mouth.

Neil presses his fingers to his lips.

Anna holds up a newspaper, points to the date and reads it. Then she sets it down on the bed beside her and picks up a plain white piece of paper, folded in quarters. "This is a list of suspects," she says without ceremony as she unfolds the paper. "Former clients of mine. I saw something in each of them that was—" Anna shakes her head and continues. "I went to the police but they didn't do anything. One of the clients is married to a judge. One of them has a brother on the police force. And the third—she's connected too. Her sister's a partner in a law firm. I know this breaks every ethical rule, recording this, but as I said, if you're watching me now, I'm dead and it was no accident."

Anna slumps her shoulders and looks off camera. She grips the piece of paper and sighs. Runs a delicate hand through her hair.

"Before I read this, I should start at the beginning. If you don't believe me—like the police didn't—investigate the people on this list." She shakes the paper. "Then decide." She glares into the camera.

"Billy, if you're watching—" Anna says, as if she's just remembered something, "Please know I was just trying to protect you. It's a wonderful thing that you never believed me—believed in my—abilities. I just wanted you to be safe. After all you've already been through. After all you've done for Deepak and me."

Neil and I look at Billy, who is staring at the screen and nodding, as if he finally understands everything Anna's ever tried to explain. His face is stricken, as if an avalanche of tears is pushed up against his skin, pressing for release.

"When I was six years old," Anna says, "I saw my grand-mother's thoughts for the first time. We were sitting in my mother's kitchen playing Old Maid and I knew what her card was before she put it down. I could see a purplish glow around her body that I later learned was her aura. That was the beginning. As I grew up, I learned how to tune in to people's thoughts, read auras, and eventually help to heal them. I could send them images. Which I learned is very rare. Obviously very few people in the world can do any of this. There are groups. Meetings. Seminars. Nobody really knows we exist. We are pacifists for the most part. The government has tried to use some of us—it didn't end well. But most people, when confronted with the truth, rationalize all sorts of ways to deny our abilities."

Anna looks like she's shaking. From fear, or anger. Probably a mixture. Then she begins to cry, reaches up a hand and turns the camera off.

Billy, Neil and I look at each other, our mouths ajar.

Neil says, "What is this about auras? I thought that was new age bullshit."

"It's not bullshit," Billy snaps. Then glances at me and corrects himself. "I mean—sorry, man," he says to Neil. "I used to think the same thing."

The screen comes to life again and Anna is there, wearing the same thing as before, in the same position, in the same room, in the same light, with the same newspaper beside her on the bed. She wipes her eyes and apologizes. The piece of paper lies in her lap. She picks it up with shaking hands and begins to read.

"One. Melanie Hoffman, Villanova. Client from April through September, 2004. Melanie terrorized her family. She killed the family dog by stabbing it to death. She said she did it to teach her children a lesson. She had terrible fantasies of slicing a puppy's throat while she forced them to watch. She constantly browsed online for puppies. I worked so hard with her on this, and I really felt we were about to have a breakthrough. But—" Anna sighs. "It kept happening. She told me to stay out of her life or she would make me sorry."

"Holy shit," Neil says. "How did she—"

Billy and I shush him.

"Two. Jessica Murray, Gladwyne. Client from October, two-thousand five through March, two-thousand six. Jessica repeatedly molested her son, starting when he was an infant. He's in school now. I have no idea if she's still—I tried to stop her. I worked with her every day. She was so ashamed. And so sorry. We worked on her compulsion. But she stopped treatment. Threatened to harm me if I kept calling. I was just thinking of her son. And her soul, you know? I can't imagine how hard it must be for her. I know she loves her son. I know it sounds ludicrous. But I know it in my heart."

Anna is openly sobbing. She pulls herself together, grabs a tissue from her night stand, blows her nose and continues.

"Three. Lacey Whitney Gould, Radnor. Client from May through June, two-thousand nine. Lacey drowned her elderly father in his bathtub, but his death was reported an accident. There was no way to go back in time obviously, but Lacey was dealing with a lot of guilt. Anger. Her father had been abusive. And there was a chance Lacey's children were in danger. I was desperate to work with her. Things started to get a little—well—I started seeing her two children in my readings—images that—flashes of rope. Pills. Water. Her kids. I promised her confidentiality. That I'd help her through everything if she would commit to working with me. The guilt from the murder compounded her stress, affected all her relationships...She was divorced, but took the kids every other weekend. The husband was pretty out of it. Wanted nothing to do with her. She had a history of mental problems. I was—I was sure I could help her."

Anna is visibly shaking now. The three of us gasp and stare at each other.

Anna stares into the distance, lost in thought. Is she aghast, the way I am, that all of these women reside in the most expensive, luxurious neighborhoods on the Main Line? Is she enraged like I am, at their level of security and protection? How could she not be? I want to drive over to Lacey's house and break her neck. And Melanie. Oh my God. And the other one too.

Neil and I glance at Billy, at the tears rolling down his face. "She must have called Lacey that night. After Julie and Deepak went to bed. She probably thought she could save her and her kids. But why couldn't I be there?" He sobs like a baby. Like my Sam does when he's in the throes of agony. Only with Sam it's usually because he doesn't have a friend to play with, or he's messed up for the third time on his homework. Billy's just—completely wrecked.

I put my hand to my mouth. I want so badly to reach my arms around him, let him know that somebody would have gotten to her sooner or later. Maybe she got off lucky. Maybe an ability like hers is better left untapped. "She wanted to keep you out of it," I say, as tenderly as I can muster.

"I miss you, Billy. Deepak. I love you guys." Anna kisses her peace fingers and touches her heart. "I didn't tell you because I was afraid. I was so scared. And there were threats. Against you, and me, and I didn't know what to do and I'm so sorry. I wanted to keep you safe. Please take this to the police. I love you." Anna reaches her hand forward and the screen freezes.

"She thinks she was the only one!" Billy wails, and a fresh wave of sobs overtakes him.

Neil turns to Billy and begins apologizing. Billy wraps his arms around Neil and the two of them hug behind my back, pitching me forward. I feel like I'm on an airplane, assuming crash position. Neil weeps into Billy's shoulder. "I'm so sorry, man," he says over and over.

"We have to go to the police right now," I say, crushed beneath the weight of this tearful bromance, my face inching closer to the floor. "And you're hurting my back."

Chapter 29

ome weeks afterward, Neil, Larry, Jeannie and I e-mail this article to each other, from the *Huffington Post*:

Philadelphia—During the autopsy of drowning victim and alleged "thoughtress" Anna Lisko, startling evidence was discovered—in the deceased's rectum. The evidence was a detailed, single-spaced letter typed in four-point font, scrolled, shrink-wrapped and stoppered with a smooth stone of polished red jasper, reported to be beneficial for the root chakra.

The letter, signed by Anna, along with her post-mortem DVD recording, further implicated three former clients, and provided disturbing details of the crimes, dates and possible locations where physical evidence could be located, based on what Anna had "seen" in her former clients' thoughts and had "read in their auras."

Mrs. Lacey Whitney Gould, 44, after eighteen hours of psychiatric evaluation and police questioning, confessed to drowning her father, Bruce Gould, in 2009.

Mrs. Gould further admitted to entering the Dorian household the evening of October 9 and, after a late-night healing treatment, drowning Anna Lisko after slipping sleeping pills and painkillers into her nightly detox smoothie. She has also confessed to the murder of Deepak Dorian, by drowning, in order to keep him from screaming and waking the nanny, who is reported to be a light sleeper. Mrs. Gould insists that she had not intended to hurt the boy.

Upon searching Mrs. Gould's Radnor mansion, numerous binders filled with newspaper clippings, diary entries and photographs of Anna Lisko were found, as well as numerous bottles of prescription-strength sleeping pills, fiber and protein supplements and painkillers. The same medications and supplements were found in the deceased's body.

Anna Lisko's other former clients are being investigated and at least one additional arrest has been made.

Mrs. Gould is still being evaluated at the Hospital of the University of Pennsylvania. Her arraignment is scheduled for Friday.

Back and forth we go online, my brother, sister and me—a merry-go-round of *yes, but how exactly?* as further information is released in spurts and dribbles—how Lacey and Anna had once been confidantes who shared diet and wellness tips, and that's how she knew how to tamper with the smoothie. And how Lacey must have arrived just as Rick's cherry-red pick-up truck was departing— how she must have seen Anna and Rick, because this information eventually became public and thrust his and Anna's affair into the spotlight, undermining Anna's credibility as a healer, but also resulting in Rick's second divorce, from a Beth who couldn't bear to wear blinders anymore. An article from *Gawker* held a special place in our sent folders and in-boxes:

Billy Dorian's name has finally been cleared and the storm surrounding his family's legacy of rage and violence has tempered significantly, with one exception: Rick Dorian Jr., who is now battling a divorce from his wife, Beth.

Rick Jr. has been residing in Atlantic City since Lacey Whitney Gould's testimony was released and leaked in part on the

Internet. The elder Dorian sibling has been witnessed in numerous casinos, according to police reports, and has been arrested twice for drunk and disorderly conduct. His contracting business, Dorian Construction, filed for bankruptcy on February 10.

While the news is good for Billy Dorian, the events surrounding the drownings and related crimes have further ignited the nation's paranoia regarding safety—*How well do you* really *know your neighbors?* The ladies on The View and other morning talk shows want to know.

They, and we here at Huffington Post, hope you know exactly—who are the people in your neighborhood, so you can avoid being a victim of violent crime. And please, if you see or hear anything suspicious, contact your local authorities.

A lot of good that did for Anna, may she rest in peace.

Chapter 30

I'm in an MRI machine. I must lie perfectly still for twenty minutes while technicians photograph my lumbar spine. Sharp beeps like car alarms blaze through my skull even though they've given me headphones; I can barely hear Coldplay through the cacophony. Tears slide into my ears. I have to cough, but if I do they'll need to start all over. I lie frozen in this magnetic coffin for what feels like forever as my spine is photographed and captured from the inside out. Nausea blooms in my gut and I swallow. I cannot erase what's happened between Billy and me, and I cannot undo the wreckage of my marriage, but I can keep going, one breath at a time, and see where it leads me.

Back at home I tape the X-rays to the lamps in my room so they glow like Halloween decorations. The IUD I had inserted after Chloe was born, right around the time the pain started, is like a neon arrow beneath my pelvis, pointing the way to my crotch like it's an after-hours tavern. The haughty brightness of it compared to the ghostly blocks of my vertebrae vexes me like a schoolyard prank. I didn't expect to see that little scribble of white there. I barely remember its existence most days, even though it's always with me. It makes me wonder if I could forget Billy one day, if his stunning perfection will dull from a dazzling glow to a mere spot of silver in the corner of my eye, like a ghost.

The chemical smell of the MRI paper stings my nostrils as I spread the giant sheets across my bed. I peer at them as if I'm trying to decipher Mandarin, then grab my laptop and locate a website devoted to helping laypeople interpret their MRIs and X-rays.

I've got a bulging disc, in a typical spot, between my L5 and the first vertebrae of my sacrum. With help from the website, I locate it on the glossy paper among a dozen identical-seeming snapshot slices of my spine—a gray blob oozing out of its kidney-shaped perimeter. There are other findings too, listed without ceremony on my report—bone spurring, stenosis, spondylosis. I Google all the words and learn that I am arthritic, with a narrowed spinal canal that could impinge on certain nerves. I sit up as if listening for the pain, waiting for the sensation in my back to grow intense with this new information. I sit in the silence, and wait.

Some time later Neil comes upstairs. Looks at me. I can tell without having to read his mind that it's time for us to talk. We begin at nine and stay up well past midnight, revealing everything—the bad, the ugly, the adulterous. This time there are no weepy apologies. Just sober facts and a dawning realization that despite it all, we want to stay together, and not just for the sake of the bank account, or the children. We've been through too much together. And we are growing old together whether we like it or not. When he asks me why I don't leave him for Billy I tell him the truth: Billy gave me what I needed, but he's not what I need. Neil thought this made sense and did not ask me to elaborate. I thought about it a lot after Anna's case was resolved. I imagined leaving my family and moving to Mount Airy to be with Billy. Uprooting the kids, living with a healer whose past is so dark and violent that it's created in him a compulsion to crusade for detachment. As much as I admire his strength and fortitude, as well as his amazing body and practiced hands, it would not work in the end. He doesn't need me or my children complicating his resolve. I will miss him, but realize that I'd miss Neil and the kids more. And my mother is right. They need us together under the same roof. For better or for worse, we are a family. And now that we've both strayed, the time is upon me to forgive him.

"Did you see?" Neil asks, pointing toward the window as the sun starts to make its way into the eastern sky. We walk over to the window and look at the neighbor's house. A For Sale sign is staked in the yard. Neil takes my hand and looks at me. "It's not supposed to be easy," he says, echoing my mother's wisdom.

Holding hands, we watch the sunrise over the expensive slate roof next door.

When Neil starts a new day job in March we crawl into bed together at ten o'clock, relishing the novelty of such a mundane occurrence. I burrow into the side of his body, rejoice in his warmth, and especially his forgiveness. Spooned within him, I clasp my hands together, grateful that somehow he sees the good in me still. I pray that his forgiveness can be like a rope pulling our marriage to safety, or thread that can stitch the pieces of our hearts back together. *Thankyouthankyou*, I mouth, pressing my body closer to his.

One night my mother holds out her arms and I step into her embrace and notice how childlike I feel there, how loved and safe and accepted, the way I used to feel, when things like rain, and mud, and splashing in puddles were fun for me. She whispers in my ear that she loves me, that she always knew I would do the right thing, make the intelligent choice. *Kene hora poo poo poo*, she says, and huffs my hair like glue. Even if she thinks I'm a fat slut, it's nothing I haven't thought about myself a million times before. She knows my deepest shame, and loves me anyway.

Neil and I sit facing each other at a new restaurant near our house, hung with giant color photos of Indian markets, with an exposed kitchen. We share a plate of chicken tikka masala and saag paneer. There is no pressure to love the meal, to love each other, so we are filled with the stuff, as sweet and creamy as the dishes set before us. We don't do much talking but when we do it is light and airy like the pockets of steam rising from our fluffy poori. We talk about the children mostly, Sam's burgeoning sarcastic streak and his new ability to sit still for longer periods of time. Chloe's growing fascination with the vacuum cleaner, her habit of spending fifteen minutes at a time in the bathroom with the door closed singing made-up songs about Ariel the mermaid.

Waiting for yoga class to begin, Jeannie declares that Neil's devotion is unprecedented. "You need to hold onto him for dear life," she says, and regales me with tales of her latest tryst, with a painter who once sang in a British pop band that we both worshipped as teens.

For the first time in yoga class I choose not to extend my spine even one degree. I twist only a fraction of what I used to, unwilling to chase after yoga's healing promise, to be its bitch. I refuse to meet the pain even halfway and wonder if yoga really is a metaphor for life, and if so, if I am finally ready to stop punishing myself. After class I hug Jeannie goodbye and walk to my car, mobile, supple, loose. When my card expires I roll up my mat and stick it in a corner, trading yoga for long walks, sometimes with Neil. Sometimes with my mother or Jeannie. But most often alone.

One night I open my laptop and a story arrives as if it had been waiting. From dinner until midnight it spills out of me, and the next day, and the next. I sit at my desk, or lie in bed, or stand at the kitchen counter typing. One month passes. Then two. Then five. The kids and Neil orbit, and the seasons change, while I remain centered and sheltered within the mutable walls of an entirely new kind of obsession. As dishes collect in the sink, the laundry piles up, and crumbs and dust scatter across the floor like earthly stars, I write, until one sunny quiet morning I exhale, and write the words, *The End.*

Epilogue

~ ⌒ ⌣

3 Years Later

onight is no different than any other—the Whole Foods parking lot is a mess. Once I'm over the speed bump I head for the outer reaches—the dark, unpopular spots near the dumpsters. The rain does not deter me.

Inside the store, business-attired customers fill their black plastic baskets with tonight's dinner. The guacamole samples are turning brown and the organic raspberries have been thoroughly picked over. With minutes to spare I make my way toward the meat section, avoiding the expensive cheeses and grabbing two tubs of biodynamic whole milk yogurt on the way. A few of Those Main Line Women hover over the salad selection like bedazzled flies, picking through steel tubs of tabbouleh, curried chick peas and toasted quinoa with metal tongs that remind me of pelican beaks. Where once I would feel a stab of envy at their flashy wealth, thanks to Anna I now know for sure that we are all fucked up and that no one gets out alive. My jealousy was misguided, a mirage. We're all in this together. We all eat, sleep, shit and fuck, whether we do it in a cardboard box under a bridge or in a three-million dollar Main Line mansion.

There's a man wearing a Baby Bjorn reaching for a package of ground lamb. The baby strapped to his chest is wailing her head off, her pink leather booties jerking and kicking. The man bounces lightly on his toes and shushes the baby gently. I watch from behind, grateful I am long-done with that wordlessly confusing phase of my children's lives. When he turns around I see that it's Billy.

"Eve?" he says, his mouth widening into a surprised smile, eyebrows arching. The baby stops crying long enough to look at my face, but her bottom lip remains curled like a potato chip. There are two glaring differences between the Billy I once lusted after and the one I see before me, and I can't say I'm not heartened in some way about it. For one, his hair is shaved clean down to his skull; and two, his once silk-smooth demeanor appears snagged and frayed with the responsibility parenthood brings—the domestic bondage you cannot ever prepare for, that no one can adequately warn you about, even if you raised your nephew as your own son for a fraction of a lifetime.

"Uh, hi," I say. "Who've you got there?" I point at the baby, who follows my finger with her shining blue eyes, distracted momentarily from her tantrum. Her face is wet and red beneath a wooly cap.

"This is Mia. She's actually five months old today. Aren't you, Sweetie?" Billy holds one of Mia's little hands. I watch the baby's fingers grasp Billy's pointer finger, one of the fingers that kneaded my flesh once upon a time. Neil and I thought about Mia for a name for our daughter. I remember what it means—*mine*. The perfect name for Billy's girl.

"Happy birthday, Mia!" I say to the baby, leaning close to her round little face. She smiles, revealing the white kernel of a first tooth.

"We're just out grabbing some dinner," Billy explains.

"I see. Well, congratulations. She's really beautiful." I imagine the mother must be beautiful too. I wonder what her childhood was like. Or if she felt like she won the lottery the first time Billy kissed her.

"Thanks," he says.

We nod and smile at each other, behold each other, and then stare at the floor. I scan the shelves and then grab two packages of grass-fed lamb chops. "Well, it was great seeing you," I say. "And she's really beautiful. I'm happy for you."

"Thanks Eve. It's good to see you too. And oh! Hey. I read your book. It was *very* interesting. Congratulations on publishing."

I feel my face flush. I bite my lip. "Thank you." I say. "I really appreciate it."

"I liked the healer character," he says. Then he whispers, "He was *exquisite.*"

I burst out laughing, and then we stand there speechless, maybe remembering all that's transpired between us.

"Did you ever find any time to write?" I ask.

He gestures to the baby and shrugs. "Next life, maybe," he says, which makes us both smile.

"Well, it was great running into you," I say, allowing my eyes to linger a moment more. *He is still breathtaking,* I think.

"You too," he says, and I peer at him, unsure if he's responding to what I've said, or what I've thought. Maybe it doesn't matter.

Mia stuffs her little hand into her mouth. She drools with delight and shrieks. Billy's eyebrows raise, amused, apologetic. He clutches his shopping basket and smiles one more time.

"Okay, see you," I say and head to the checkout counter. On my way back to the minivan where Neil and the kids are waiting, I turn my face toward the sky and walk slowly through the falling rain, allowing myself to get sopping, soaking wet.

Acknowledgments

Thank you to Bill, Marci, Billy and Ricky McDermott for the deer hunting expedition and support (my ass is still frozen), my agent Jennifer Unter and the SparkPress team—Crystal Patriarche, Lauren Wise, Brooke Warner, Robert Soares, Hanna Sichting, Julie Metz, Katherine Lloyd, and Chris Dumas. Thank you Eleanor Abrams, Bryan, Ry and Frankie Miller for inspiring, encouraging and putting up with me, friends and avid supporters Marti Keegan, Michelle Collier, Chris Dorian, Sarah Barr, and Alicia Kopp, and Anne Tetreault of the Spiral Bookcase.

About the Author

 Elise A. Miller is the author of the satirical romance *Star Craving Mad.* Her work has appeared in the anthology *Because I Love Her,* at nerve.com and freshyarn.com, and in the *Northern Liberties Review, Elephant Journal,* and *Schuylkill Valley Journal.* Miller is also an SFG kettlebell instructor and fitness trainer, as well as a creative writing coach and editor. She lives in Lower Merion, Pennsylvania with one husband, two kids, two dogs, and one constantly shedding wool shag rug.

SELECTED TITLES FROM SPARKPRESS

SparkPress is an independent boutique publisher delivering high-quality, entertaining, and engaging content that enhances readers' lives.
Visit us at www.gosparkpress.com

Star Craving Mad, by Elise Miller. $17, 978-1-94071-673-2. A middle-aged elite private elementary school teacher's life changes when her celebrity fantasy becomes a reality.

The Goodbye Year, by Kaira Rouda. $17, 978-1-940716-33-6. Told from the points of view of both the parents and kids, *The Goodbye Year* explores high school peer pressure, what it's like for young people to face the unknown of life after high school, and how a transition that should be the beginning of a parents' second act together—empty nesting—is often actually the end.

The House of Bradbury, by Nicole Meier. $17, 978-1-940716-38-1. After Mia Gladwell's debut novel bombs and her fiancé jumps ship, she purchases the estate of iconic author Ray Bradbury, hoping it will inspire her best work yet. But between her disapproving sister, mysterious sketches that show up on her door, and taking in a pill-popping starlet as a tenant—a favor to her needy ex—life in the Bradbury house is not what she imagined.

So Close, by Emma McLaughlin and Nicola Kraus. $17, 978-1-940716-76-3. A story about a girl from the trailer parks of Florida and the two powerful men who shape her life—one of whom will raise her up to places she never imagined, the other who will threaten to destroy her. Can a girl like her make it to the White House? When her loyalty is tested will she save the only family member she's ever known—even if it means keeping a terrible secret from the American people?

ABOUT SPARKPRESS

SparkPress is an independent, hybrid imprint focused on merging the best of the traditional publishing model with new and innovative strategies. We deliver high-quality, entertaining, and engaging content that enhances readers' lives. We are proud to bring to market a list of *New York Times* bestselling, award-winning, and debut authors who represent a wide array of genres, as well as our established, industry-wide reputation for innovative, creative, results-driven success in working with authors. SparkPress, a BookSparks imprint, is a division of SparkPoint Studio, LLC.

Learn more at GoSparkPress.com